An Enemy n View

by David Hoffman

Published by

GENERAL STORE
PUBLISHING HOUSE

Box 28, 1694B Burnstown Road
Burnstown, Ontario, Canada K0J 1G0
Telephone (613) 432–7697 or 1–800–465–6072

ISBN 1–894263–72–3
Printed and bound in Canada

Design and layout by Leanne Enright
Cover artwork by Tim Yearington
Author photo by Ron DeVries
Cover design by Taragraphics
Printing by Custom Printers of Renfrew Ltd.

Copyright © 2002
General Store Publishing House
Burnstown, Ontario, Canada

Canadian Cataloguing in Publication Data

Hoffman, David, 1936–
    An enemy in view / David Hoffman.
ISBN 1–894263–72–3

    I. Title.

PS8565.O332E54 2002   C813'.6   C2002-903340-3
PR9199.4.H63E54 2002

For my family

ACKNOWLEDGEMENTS

It takes both encouragement and unvarnished honesty in friends and editors to get the job done. I have Sheila Reeser to thank for a critical but, in the end, productive review of the first draft, and George Grennel for many helpful suggestions on both the first and second. Together they gave me the courage to continue. Gary, Cathryn, and Laura Hoffman all sustained my imagination, and my wife, Katie, gave me the unreserved support I needed throughout.

As I grew closer to my goal, Susan Code McDougall, my editor, inspired the hope that the end was achievable, and prodded and polished my effort when I flagged. James Hurley kindly inspected several key chapters in which the public service setting was important and saved me from a few gaffes. Ron DeVries took the photos that inspired the cover concept.

Although references to real people and places abound, this is a pure piece of fiction in which all the characters have lived only in my head. None enjoy—or have ever had—the pleasure of a paycheque from a newspaper, university, or government department.

"Nothing would more contribute to make a man wise than to have always an enemy in view."

—Lord Halifax (1881–1959), U.K. Foreign Secretary

CHAPTER 1

If you're going to mount a long ladder, his father used to say, you'd better be sure of all the rungs before you start. Charles Haversham, who often thought he knew better, had long ago forgotten his father's advice. This morning, he hardly had to worry about falling off a ladder. Charles was barely off the ground. Although he had not yet touched a file or drafted a memo, he already rated his workday only a two on a scale of one to ten.

A phone message from an unexpected source had greeted him when he reached his office door. André Brisson, an official in the Auditor General's Office, someone completely unknown to him, had requested a return call as soon as possible. And the briefing he had expected to give at two o'clock had been advanced to ten.

None of this was welcome now. Charles could manage—barely—the hasty preparation for the rescheduled meeting. His tongue was still too thick for an intelligent conversation. Slowly he sipped on his third cup of coffee of the morning and strained to construct some order from the buzz going on in his head.

Although he liked to pretend his Monday morning headaches sprang from tension from his job, an old-fashioned hangover was a more accurate description of the cause. Last night, he and Diane had polished off a 26'er of Scotch. A smooth single malt—for the first few drinks, at least. Before the flavour lost its edge. Before seeking pleasure changed to finding oblivion. "Getting smashed"—the expression they both recalled their parents using—had become about the only thing the couple now had in common.

Holding his head in his hands, Charles stared blankly at his empty desk. If he could not generate enough energy to move forward, he would consider what good might come from mulling over the past. His thoughts went back to a time before binge drinking had become a pattern.

Diane had begun to sneak a drink or two during the day about a year after their move to Ottawa. Charles was sure their daughter Linda had just started junior kindergarten. At first, he chose not to let on he knew, concerned with what might come out if he broached the subject. However, he did not have to wait many months for an explosion that exposed the weaknesses in their relationship, patched over with bits and pieces, which inevitably failed in even the mildest storm. As she had done before—the first occasion not long after their wedding—Diane had worked through a whole litany of wrongs to arrive at her ultimate solution for every disappointment in the marriage—divorce.

Her husband's failure to fulfill his early promise and to rise rapidly in the Ottawa public service was especially galling. Making matters worse was her own sacrifice of a successful publishing career in Toronto to the now much-regretted decision to follow Charles's star. Never one to forgive herself or anyone else easily, she admitted to wallowing for a while in self-pity. Soon, this had given way to antagonism and finally depression. Only a clean break, she had often said, held any hope for personal renewal. Yet she had hung on. As Charles had hung on.

Charles had concluded months ago that he did not have to join his wife in her binges. He generally did well during the week, when demands of the office overcame his tendency to drift. Long weekends together proved more difficult, however, and last night—as had happened more than once since the family's summer vacation—he'd become a willing accomplice in another flight into blackout.

For that excess, Charles now paid a heavy price. He glanced at his watch. Headache or no headache, he could no longer procrastinate. He bent down to take a fresh notepad from the lower drawer of his desk, his head spinning from the exertion. It was then that André Brisson, a public servant three levels from the top in the Auditor General's Office, phoned for a second time that morning.

Among a team of accountants and analysts reputed for their skills with broadswords and rapiers, André Brisson was known in the office as "Monsieur Smoothie." Steeped in internal audit procedures of a number of departments before joining the Auditor General, he had become the point man on fashioning difficult compromises—the one to draft the auditor's response when departments tell their side of the story in the Auditor General's annual reports to the House of Commons. Typically dressed in a pin-striped, dark suit and sporting a pencil-thin moustache, Brisson resembled more a funeral director from his hometown of Rimouski than a man who had worked his way up the ranks of the public service. Rumour had it, in fact, that despite his nice guy image, he'd seen to the burial of a number of departmental auditors over the years.

Ignoring Charles's feeble excuses for not returning his call immediately, Brisson went straight to his message after only the most basic of introductions.

"My group 'ad responsibility of an audit of the foreign affairs department's embassies and missions in Central America and the Caribbean," the audit principal said. "The boss decided it was time, you know, to examine dem. We sent one of our best men, Jim Shaw, to direct an intensive audit of a few of our missions. Jim discovered something in dossiers in the Barbados office dat does not make sense to us. I t'ought you might be able to assist."

Even in his foggy condition, Charles could tell the speaker was well rehearsed. *Why me? Why now?*

At Industry Canada, during the three years he was responsible for Defence Production programs, Charles often had to cope with one review or another. If it wasn't a bloody internal audit, there was somebody from program evaluation sniffing around. This had been going on ever since the Liberals, then the Opposition, had so savagely criticized the Auditor General's value-for-money audit of the Defence Industries Support Program. "Matters of continuing interest," as the AG so coyly put it.

It was not like the AG to spend much time on audits of the Privy Council Office. Besides, Charles had moved to the PCO less than two months ago. To the annoyance of senior officials at Foreign Affairs and International Trade, who would have wished their own man to fill the job, it was Charles—a director in a rival department, Industry Canada—who was transferred to the Privy Council Office within weeks of the Prime Minister's return, press-battered from his failed "Captain Canada" trade mission to South America.

Charles's main task as Special Adviser (Operations) was to assure the PM's handlers that, "Next time, nobody so much as hints at a trade mission until the deals are signed, sealed and delivered in advance." Charles Haversham was not going to make policy, but he was responsible for ensuring whatever policy there was would be consistent and properly co-ordinated. Between missions, he'd have a watching brief on developments affecting Canada's competitiveness in a global economy. Charles was only beginning to feel his way into a new job. What did he know? How could he help?

Brisson came to the heart of his subject. "You may remember," he said, "several months ago newspapers were agitated over results of an Access to Information request for records of travel expenses of all senior departmental officials. It started wit' excitement over the Language Commissioner's bills for an international conference in Lausanne. It became a search and destroy mission, you know, across all the department and agency."

"Yes, I remember that one," Charles said, his neurons firing more quickly now. "The government blinked and committed to providing everything on travel expenses of more than fifteen hundred dollars taking place over a two-year period. It must've taken months to respond."

"Dat is correct. It took a certain period of time, but finally they had a figure they could report. We were to verify detail of the backgrounder to the government press release," Brisson continued. "It provided names and total expenses for everything over the set limit. We checked the match of the master list against all internal audit files. Jim Shaw aut'orize the final release."

Charles had no idea where this was headed. Of course, he recalled the panic that the expenses issue had caused among some of his departmental colleagues. He had always considered himself a straight shooter where expenses were concerned. As a junior reporter at the *Toronto Star*, he had learned to justify every nickel and dime. The habit stuck, so that when he joined the federal public service, he handled his expense account charges in a way that set him far apart from many of his free-spending superiors. *What the hell's this got to do with me? I'm clean.*

"When de Privy Council Office submit its travel expenses for the Access request," Brisson went on, "they sent receipts for Dan Carpenter for an official visit to Washington over the weekend of December 7 and 8. Everything had documents, including the rental car and mileage allowance."

"So?"

"This we don't understand," Brisson said. "The audit of Foreign Affairs' Barbados office placed Carpenter in Barbados in a meeting at the 'Ighland Sands Resort. At the same time as his receipts show he was in Washington. Other submissions of travel expense claims by the Privy Council Office indicate that no one from PCO attend the Barbados meeting at that time. Why would Monsieur Carpenter . . . *truque* . . . er . . . fake the details of the trip? How could he fake them? The receipts and expenses look legitimate and he cannot 'ave been in two place at the same moment. None of this has sense. What do you think is going on here?"

"I have no idea," Charles said. "Besides, I don't understand why you're calling me. Dan worked with me at Industry for a while after I first went there, that's true, but he'd been in two other sections of the department before coming here."

"Yes, dat may be," Brisson responded immediately, as if his attempted evasion had been fully anticipated, "but we need someone who *knows* Carpenter and is working with him in the Privy Council Office *now* . . . an insider to survey the office so it will not arouse suspicions. That can help us to decide, you know, if we should take it further. Carpenter is, as they say, an 'igh flyer . . . with—"

"Friends in the right places, and you'd rather have me risk my ass than launch a formal inquiry that could hurt your office if it turns up nothing. Is that it?"

"Somet'ing like that," Brisson replied. "Me, I'm taking a chance with dis one, but I know you are a friend of Dan Carpenter."

"How the hell do you know that?"

"It does not matter, does it? The fact is it is so. That is why I t'ought of asking you to help, to see if you can clear this up before it becomes visible. My boss, you know, is putting the pressure on me to launch a more formal investigation—he has given me ten days to report back—and I t'ought we might avoid this if—"

"There has to be something else going on here," Charles asserted.

"In reality there is more than I told you to this point," Brisson admitted.

"Why did I think there might be?" Charles had to admire Brisson's skilful execution of duty.

Brisson continued, ignoring his sarcasm. "Dan Carpenter's expenses are only one of many we are investigating from about the same period of time. Some other *invités* . . . some surprising participants . . . were in Barbados. Apparently one of them never appeared. We have some informations. We would like to know more."

"This is not my forte," Charles said, his throat parched, his voice cracking and unassertive. He sipped the dregs of his bitter coffee.

Brisson charged on. "No concern. My staff will assemble a full package of documents. I will send them by messenger tomorrow morning. Consider carefully what you know of Carpenter's 'abits and see what you conclude from our documents. Tell no one of this request. And keep your eyes open if you get a chance to examine Carpenter's files."

Consider his habits. What does he have in mind?

Brisson gave Charles no time to pursue the thought. With deliberate finality, he completed his mission. "Let my secretary know when you 'ave something to report and I will arrange for our *rendez-vous clandestine . . .* if that is not too dramatic a word. You will be discrete, of course. We are not to ruffle feathers."

"Of course not."

"Bonne chance!"

"Sure."

Charles removed his glasses, rubbed his thumbs into his eyeballs until they hurt, and tilted his head back as far as his office chair would allow. At that moment, he felt more like a public servant about to be put out to pasture than a vigorous baby boomer in the habit of jogging to work many mornings. Why in God's name wouldn't Brisson have simply asked Dan's boss, Roger Lavigne? Was Brisson genuinely trying to save Dan from possible embarrassment? Or was he cleverly exploiting a natural desire to try to protect a friend and, in the process, get him to do the AG's work?

Charles was uncomfortable. It was more than the hangover. Even if he played up the positive side of the task, which Brisson had emphasized, the actions he now felt coerced into carrying out ran completely against form. He hated the idea of spying on a colleague, especially one he knew well and liked. Besides, he was no great admirer of the government's auditor. (Too prone, Charles always considered, to mess with what were properly political decisions and then blame public servants for the results.)

If pushed, Charles had to admit he was the tiniest bit envious of his younger friend's fast track up the ranks. After all, Dan had been *his* junior research officer a scant six years ago. On the other hand, his own recent shift to PCO was concrete recognition of his abilities. He had been looking for a chance to move into the limelight for some time. The PCO position was a good start. But, doing a dirty job for the Auditor General's Office was not what he had in mind.

Regarded from the start by his peers as solidly competent, Charles had made his early mark crafting clever words for his superiors: solid background research and clearly expressed memos and press releases that advanced his department's cause or diverted suspicious critics. These had been the keys to the initial success of his public service career, much of it traceable to analytical and writing skills honed by ten years' experience as a political reporter.

Not that his résumé was limited to a career in journalism. A few years' apprenticeship in the Southam chain, and a long stint on the parliamentary desk for the *Toronto Star*, had gained Charles the Alexander Prize for Journalistic Excellence. This prize offered him a year's sabbatical in any university course of his choosing and, without a moment's hesitation, he had enrolled in the Masters Program in Business Administration at the University of Toronto.

Fascination with the exercise of power at the political and bureaucratic level in Ottawa drove his decision. An MBA, better even than articling with a top law firm, seemed the quickest way up in Ottawa. Although a degree from Harvard was the surest route, choosing that school would have meant separation from Diane at a time when their marriage was already shaky. Unwilling to face that prospect while trying to make the most of his sabbatical, Charles refused to question his choice. He committed fully to his studies, determined to benefit to the fullest from his opportunity.

Charles soon caught the attention of his senior professors. Seymour Bart, Professor of International Trade and Investment, was particularly impressed. A shrewd businessman and respected scholar, Bart moved with equal ease in the boardrooms of international business and the upper echelons of university administration. In the 1970s, Bart had even been considered a serious prospect for the university presidency. However, unease with his origins within Toronto's old money elite and opposition from a rag-tag group of leftist faculty because of his evident cosiness with Bay Street combined to stymie Bart's chances.

After a short-lived, self-imposed exile as Deputy Minister of Trade and Commerce in Ottawa, Bart had returned refreshed to his university role. Credited with connections that would-be rivals could merely dream of, Bart soon consolidated his already formidable reputation as trusted adviser to the country's most successful CEOs. The result was a happy reciprocity, both personally and for the university.

Bart began to amass a retirement fund, as he liked to call it, that was the envy of his less well-positioned colleagues; and his students benefited from the freshness and richness of real-life business decision-making that Bart was able to bring to his classroom. The university, relishing the prestige that adhered to the institution from Bart's informal gathering of business friends, found the means to house within the business school the offices of what came to be known as "The Group." Like Juan Antonio Samaranch during his long stint with the International Olympic Committee, Bart selected its members and controlled every aspect of its investment activities.

As Charles's reflective mood absorbed him, he went back to a day when Seymour Bart had made him an offer that was to shape his career profoundly.

Although he could not recall now whether Bart had ever spoken to him before that occasion, except in the seminar room, Charles had a clear fix on the day the professor invited him to his office. He had liked Bart's directness: "Maybe it has to do with your age and experience compared to your classmates, but I was struck by the acuity of your analysis of the Canadian Pacific/Grover Bay merger case in last week's seminar. How on earth did you put together enough of the story—I assume with no direct help from the inside—to pull off such an insightful piece of analysis?"

"I suppose it depends on what you mean by direct help," Charles had replied. He'd explained that he never saw any private documentation, company memos or anything like that; although he did get a few clues from talking with a friend in the business news section of the *Star* and from interviewing accountants working for both firms on a not-for-attribution basis.

"Imagine," the professor had said, "what you could do with real insider information." It was this thought that had brought Bart to the point of inviting Charles to his office.

"I've a proposal to put to you that has all the flavour of a mutually satisfactory *quid pro quo*," Bart had said. "I will get you a job with the Bureau of Competition Policy in Ottawa after graduation and in return I want you to do a favour for me. Let me in on whatever you learn from your next practicum assignment with Red Top Gold, the new mining consortium. Nothing risky for you, I assure you. I simply need to know a few things—like whether the board is planning an extraordinary meeting before the shareholders' meeting in June. Innocent enough in itself, but useful to my associates and me. That'll be the end of it . . . and you'll be happily launched on a fine career in the federal public service. What do you say?"

Charles had replayed the next scene in his mind many times. In some versions, he is a resolute idealist, smoothly thanking his mentor for the kind words about his latest research paper and feigning no interest in a job in Competition Policy—now or in the near future. At other times he is an eager, yet conflicted coward, wanting to take advantage of a boost, but worried about the consequences if his actions should be revealed.

Today Charles was not fooling himself. As he reflected on the soul-searching he had done before Brisson's call, and on the AG's surprising request to investigate Dan Carpenter's travel expenses, he recalled vividly the indecent haste with which he had welcomed Professor Bart's engaging proposition.

Bart had summed up their confidential chat with the old homily: "God helps those who help themselves." As soon as he had blurted out his agreement, Charles had wondered if there was not a more appropriate saying. One that starts with "The road to hell . . ."

CHAPTER 2

1

From his eleventh floor office window in the Royal Bank Centre, Dan Carpenter had a view of the renovations underway at the War Memorial in Confederation Square—Confusion Square, as Ottawa drivers know it. He thought of the prime minister's recent announcement about sending a few troops to the Balkans and the negative reaction of most of the media to the idea. It made him think of the pride with which his mother always spoke of his father's volunteering to serve in the Canadian Army in World War II.

Dan wondered if his country would ever see fit to honour its "fighting men" again. Canadians, he was convinced, had become too damn scared of taking risks for their own good. *Maybe you need to be a risk-taker yourself to appreciate risk.*

For one so young—it had been only seven years since he had received a master's degree in economics from the prestigious Massachusetts Institute of Technology—Dan had already been entrusted with substantial responsibility. At Industry Canada, he had proven to be a quick learner, an asset noticed early on by his assistant deputy minister. If he was perhaps too brashly self-confident for some of his stodgier colleagues, he overcame most people's initial negative reactions with his good looks and winning smile.

Single and to all appearances not deeply involved with anyone in particular, Dan had made a strong impression on the younger female staff at the PCO. Wiry, athletic looking and charming; more than enough, the guys in the office mail room grudgingly conceded, to get him into the pants of the best looking babes in Ottawa anytime he fancied.

They did not hire Dan, however, for his appearance. Quick yet thorough, analytical *and* persuasive (something of a rare combination in Ottawa), Dan Carpenter represented the type of person most senior managers longed to have on their policy and planning team. Fortunately for him, these qualities were soon recognized in several quarters and, at the age of thirty, Dan received an appointment to the Privy Council Office—widely regarded as a critical stepping stone to promotion to higher departmental responsibilities.

The Privy Council Office, Dan's home for more than a year, is the engine of the so-called "central agencies." It's the prime minister's own department and the secretariat to the cabinet. Working closely with the Finance Department, Treasury Board and the Prime Minister's Office, its non-elected officials steer the major policy directions of the federal government. Like a giant vacuum cleaner, the agency sucks up policy advice and information from departments, processes it, refines it, and deposits it before its political masters in a form critical to their decision-making.

Though the style of the PCO has varied over the years— determined invariably by the preferences of the prime minister and the inclination of the senior public servant in Ottawa, the clerk of the privy council—the office has always advised the prime minister on major public policy and the structure of the public service. To underscore the vital role of co-ordination and information exchange that resides in this powerful agency of about five hundred persons, the clerk of the privy council simultaneously combines the roles of deputy minister to the prime minister, secretary to the cabinet, *and* head of the public service.

Typical PCO staffers work long hours in a pressure cooker environment, one in which extraordinary commitment is expected but rewards are normally deferred for later recognition. In this respect as well, Dan was not run-of-the mill; although he always managed to appear to be on top of his job, he made it a rule to limit his workday to no more than nine hours. It was a rare situation, indeed, that forced Dan to miss a tennis match or a golf game with his friends.

Dan had been at the office since eight o'clock—earlier than usual for him—because he knew that a fair chunk of his workday would later be lost. He was committed to travelling that afternoon to Montebello to stay at a luxury resort on the Quebec side of the Ottawa River for a "strategic retreat." He would leave his office ahead of rush hour traffic, drive ninety kilometres or so east along Highways 50 and 148 and be there in time for drinks before a buffet supper and the start of the evening working session.

Roger Lavigne, Deputy Secretary (Operations), and the Privy Council Office official to whom Dan reported, was fond of having meetings with his staff away from routine pressures of phone, fax and e-mail. When Monday's executive committee meeting highlighted the need for co-ordination of new policy directions with staffing initiatives and other logistical matters, Lavigne lost no time in concluding that the situation was ripe for another of his Montebello "getaways."

"I'm inviting only a few key people," Lavigne announced to his hastily assembled staff, "and we're going to stick with the top priority issues until we have them settled—no matter how long it takes. Be prepared to stay over until Sunday morning, at all events."

Dan fingered the file prepared for the Montebello meeting lying on his desk. He shuffled the discussion papers absentmindedly, distracted by concerns seemingly more pressing than the upcoming working session. Eventually, he focused and glanced at the agenda topics. Dan tossed the papers on his desk in disgust. Considering the agenda was supposed to contain something Lavigne was all hot and bothered over, there was screw-all.

He studied the distribution list for the meeting notes again:

> Roger Lavigne, Deputy Secretary, Operations
>
> Francine Coté, Director Strategic Planning
>
> Dan Carpenter, Adviser Major Projects
>
> Fred Harris, Director Economic Planning
>
> Norman Crawley, Assistant Director Operations Liaison
>
> Charles Haversham, Special Adviser (Operations).

Coté, as far as Dan was concerned, was a natural, considering the meeting's purpose. He could not say the same for Harris. Fred could hardly ever be counted on to add anything in a meeting that he had not already said better in a memo. As for Crawley, a good man for the job, devoted to detail and all that, yet hardly somebody to contribute much to a strategic planning session like this one. The Coté-Harris-Crawley team had moved over with Lavigne shortly after he left the Department of Finance. First Harris, a few months later Coté, and finally Crawley.

Dan was not sure what position Lavigne had held at Finance, but he supposed that it had been in corporate taxation in some senior capacity. It made sense, considering Lavigne had been Executive Director of the Canadian Manufacturers Association before being parachuted into the public service on the Executive Interchange Program.

What Dan knew about Lavigne was that he was a man not to be taken lightly. In contrast to the flippant "johnny-one-notes" Dan had encountered in most of his work, Roger Lavigne presented the image of a man that time had moulded into solid bedrock. Layer upon layer of learning and experience, decision-taking and action had accumulated in one strong-willed human being, each varied stratum a resource to call upon as required. Fluently bilingual, the only child of an Edinburgh-born mother and a Montreal-born father, Lavigne appeared as a cultured person in both the manner and content of his expression. Forceful, yet never vulgar, Lavigne saw no need to name-drop to establish the authority of *his* position.

Yet, as Dan thought about the deputy secretary from the perspective of more than a year's work experience in the Privy Council Office, he now saw in Lavigne traces of contradiction. Caution—caution almost to a fault—appeared to be his personal talisman, above all else. Even a trifle insecure. Never in his speech. Or in the body language displayed in public. Inside somewhere, hidden in recesses, to emerge during private moments. Why else surround himself with staffers like Harris and Crawley, more noted for their loyalty than their talents? Dan had no explanation for this apparent quirk. His attention returned to the distribution list for Montebello.

Charles Haversham was to attend as well—his first invitation to a getaway with the inner circle. Dan was confident that, even so, Charles would likely emerge as star of the event. Though new to the PCO, Charles already had a reputation for visualizing clearly the many intricate steps necessary between policy concept and realization. Like Lavigne, he could grasp the nuances of various positions and bring the main message home to others. Haversham might have his bad days—Dan had seen these in the past. Most often, though, he hit squarely between the eyes with his exceptional analytical skills.

Dan had, in fact, been a fan of Charles from his first days at Industry. Something about Charles's blend of competence and intolerance of bureaucratic bullshit had appealed to the younger man from the beginning. Working with him had only deepened his respect. Charles represented the closest thing Dan had to a role model in Ottawa.

Dan recalled that colleagues used to say that Charles Haversham was too cynical to be recognized by superiors as the right stuff for rapid advancement, and too proud of his qualities to kiss-ass his way to promotion. With his latest appointment, Dan noted, Charles had effectively falsified that conclusion. Dan was pleased that his former director was now working in an important position at PCO.

Reluctantly, Dan turned to the set of working papers that formed part of the Montebello file. He picked up a hefty background paper, *Options for Research and Development Subsidies: Implications of Recent World Trade Organization Rulings*, drafted by his former colleagues at Industry Canada. *Options* was the one agenda item on which Lavigne expected him to make a major contribution. Dan flipped through the report, glancing at the topic sentence of each paragraph. Hardly anything new, he concluded, grateful he would require no preparation to get up to speed on this one.

All in all, the Montebello meeting would be a low-pressure event: an opportunity to coast through most agenda items and come alive only when discussion turned to how the government would support research and development in the future. It was to be a working weekend that, everything considered, suited Dan admirably.

He called in his secretary for a quick briefing on next week's events, phoned his tennis partner to cancel their Sunday morning match at the Rideau Tennis Club, and made a final check on the day's e-mails.

Before shutting down his computer, Dan completed a ritual operation: He first copied an item to a diskette, then trashed his opened e-mails. Next, he emptied the recycle bin. As he waited for the computer to shut down, Dan placed the diskette inside a soft plastic container sealed with two-sided tape. Reaching into the top left-hand drawer as far as he could with his arm, he pressed the package to the roof of the underside of his desk. Then he knelt down and inspected the result. Satisfied with its firm attachment, Dan gently closed the drawer.

He might have locked his desk with the key he had inherited from an office predecessor, but Dan chose not to. As he flicked off his desk lamp, he thought briefly about the contents of the diskette. Then he shrugged. For Dan, taking risks had become a way of life.

2

The package from André Brisson's office—marked "Recipient's Eyes Only"—had been sitting in Charles's locked filing cabinet since it had been delivered on Tuesday. It was now Friday afternoon, and Charles had just returned from an unusually long lunch. He thought it might be time to move Brisson's missive to the corner of his desk, at least. More than that, he was still unable to do.

Each time Charles felt the slightest inclination to satisfy his curiosity, he would move the envelope further from his grasp, as if to assert—retroactively—his determination not to cave in to the request of the Office of the Auditor General. For the longest time he resisted even opening the package, favouring instead some trivial piece of correspondence, or his notes for the Montebello getaway. Charles found his concentration wandering.

From his north-facing window, Charles could see only the top of the tower of the Parliament Buildings, his line of sight partially blocked by the Blackburn Building, home of many other officials in the Privy Council Office. Between his new workplace and Parliament lay the brown stone solidity of the Langevin Block. There, the secretary to the cabinet and an inner circle of deputy secretaries—public servants all, sharing space with the unelected appointees in the Prime Minister's Office—labour each day in support of the prime minister and the government of Canada. Roger Lavigne had his office on the east side of the third floor of the Langevin, one staircase away from a senior adviser in the PMO.

Charles found it ironic how fiercely he now longed for an office in the Langevin Block. It was more than a question of convenience— although it was a pain for him to have to leave his building, walk a block and climb to the third floor whenever Lavigne summoned. No, being inside the Langevin was a mark of prestige, a symbol— reserved for a fortunate few—of achievement in a bureaucracy famous for its minute distinctions of rank. While Charles was conscious that he had worked for years in other departments in Ottawa completely indifferent to the minutiae of officialdom's class structure, after only a few weeks in his new position in the Privy Council Office, he already held a PhD in the science of rug-ranking.

As a political reporter with the *Toronto Star*, he had had little time for senior civil servants in general and almost none for the tight-lipped policy analysts that dominated the PCO. Most of the time, "exempt staff"—like executive assistants in departmental ministers' offices or the spin-doctors in the Prime Minister's Office— provided a better place to start your story.

Charles had a different perspective now. From his vantage point on the inside, he could see that the long-standing distinction between politicos and public servants had become blurred. Certainly, the vast majority of his new colleagues in Ottawa played the game as it was always played—respectful of the line between the rulers and their advisers. But the previous government's destructive suspicion of the senior levels of the civil service, built up over years of Liberal administrations, had resulted in a transformation, a rooting out of the custodians of the old values, and the rise to influence—here and there across the federal system—of two new types of public servant: those who saw themselves unreservedly as part of the political power structure, and those who hated what they found around them so much they did not hesitate to leak documents and otherwise raise hell whenever their sensibilities on some public policy issue were aroused. As an ex-journalist, Charles had to admit the current environment offered more scope for old-fashioned, muckraking journalism.

This last thought brought him back abruptly to the task still facing him that afternoon. He ran his hands through his long black hair, now flecked with a distinguished hint of grey, expelling a deep breath at the same time. Then he rose from his chair and went to the window. For a long while he observed what looked like an argument between two beggars in the street below. Then, when that was resolved without punches thrown, he shifted his attention to a newspaper blowing in circles near the doorway of a nearby building.

Not only reluctance to follow Brisson's bidding kept him from the AG's file. Charles might contend that he would dislike the idea of snooping as much if it was anyone else in the Privy Council Office, but deep down he knew that was not so. Dan was a friend. A protégé, no less. For Brisson to expect his prompt attention to the AG's request in this case was arrogant presumption.

Charles had convinced himself that the AG must be wrong in thinking that Dan could be involved in anything more serious than some bureaucratic screw-up, an easily explained oversight by one of the PCO administrative staff. He'd seen the AG blow things up out of proportion before. He was sure this was one of those cases.

By mid-afternoon, he had run out of reasons for ignoring the AG's package. He resented the position Brisson had put him in, but he now felt he had no choice except to go ahead. There was the matter of urgency Brisson had mentioned. And the chance that he'd come up with something that would kill further interest in Dan's expense account right in its tracks. He would look at the file, determine the minimum effort necessary to satisfy the request, and get on with his life. Slitting open the double envelope protecting the contents, he leaned back in his chair. Charles had scanned only the first document when the phone rang.

"Nice to know you have a phone, at least, in your new job," said a woman at the other end. "What's the matter, Charles, forgotten how to dial?"

"I'm sorry," he blurted, "I'm not sure I know who's calling."

"Get a lot of calls from women whose voice you don't remember, do you Charles? Try Vancouver. Try the Fountain Room of the Hyatt on a Saturday night nearly three months ago. Try a soppy woman who was impressed with the speech you made that day, and got too carried away—"

"Joan," Charles said, his intonation between a question and an assertion.

"Good guess . . . you bastard!"

"Look, Joan," he countered, trying to offset his aggressor's advantage in surprise. "I've been incredibly busy since they brought me over here . . . I haven't been out of Ottawa a single day and . . . there's been no chance to see you. I'm sorry if I led you to think that—"

"Oh, cut the horseshit, Charles, I don't blame you so much for your bang 'em and leave 'em attitude. But I do think a little thank-you call would have been considerate. After all, it's clear to me—as I would have thought it is to you—that you owe your new position at PCO largely to me."

Charles was about to compound the affront by denying all knowledge of his caller's suggestion, when the light bulb finally went on. A casual exchange in the midst of a cuddling session had taken on far more significance than he could have imagined at the time. He reached back to fill in the details.

He and Joan Macdonald, a political reporter for the *Vancouver Sun* and—when in Ottawa—occasional bed partner of Andrew Creely, recently appointed Associate Deputy Minister of Industry Canada, had spent some time together in a Vancouver hotel room. The Creely-Macdonald affair had been an on-again off-again thing for more than four years and, for all their effort to conceal it, Charles had heard of it from sources in Industry at least three years ago. The Haversham-Macdonald affair was a one-night stand, nothing more.

The Western Canada Trade Association had conscripted Charles as a substitute speaker at their annual meeting, replacing the ailing associate deputy in his department on short notice. The stand-in had made what was by all accounts an excellent speech, but it had been in the informal question and answer period afterwards that Charles had caught the reporter's attention.

The reporter, it turned out, saw in Charles a source for a feature story. She needed deep background on the pre-trip preparations for the type of high-level trade missions that had become a ritual in recent years. She meant the ones where the Canadian prime minister and the provincial premiers—in the most evident display of federal-provincial co-operation—co-ordinate their holiday travel schedules every two years and take off around the globe, pretending for a week or so to be captains of industry.

Charles's expertise fitted her requirements perfectly. The fact that she found him intellectually and physically appealing didn't hurt. That she was staring a disappointing, lonely evening in the face, instead of a liaison with her visiting lover, may have contributed even more to the outcome. Joan Macdonald, a feisty newspaperwoman originally from Cape Breton, was not a shy type. She wasted no time in suggesting a mix of business and pleasure for the evening that had Charles's attention from the get-go. That night Charles had no agenda of his own; he was content to see how the scene played out with a woman in the driver's seat.

"So you took me seriously," Charles said, "when I went on about how I'd welcome a chance to set up the Team Canada tours properly."

"It looks as if *I* took you a hell of a lot more seriously than you took me, Charlie," Joan said. "But you did get my attention," she said, softening. "I think you know that, Charles, and when I had an opportunity to whisper your name in the ear of a guy who was in a position to do something about it . . . well, I mentioned you for the job when it came up."

Charles was not sure, now, how he felt about this news. On the one hand, he was pleased that Joan had mentioned his credentials to his associate deputy. On the other, learning now of the leg-up she had given him in getting the job diminished the achievement in his own eyes. Charles had a choice: He could allow himself to get upset that the upper hierarchy had not recognized his abilities— unaided—or he could retreat to the view, heard among officials at his level, that most senior bureaucrats were so preoccupied with trying to figure out what they were supposed to be doing that they couldn't recognize real ability in others if they tripped over it.

For a second, he wondered if his wife might have been right all along about his ineffectiveness in Ottawa. After all, hadn't it been much the same with Professor Bart's assistance with an appointment to the Competition Bureau? Was that simply good luck? Or a helping hand to someone obviously in need?

For Charles, while self-doubt was a frequent visitor, its stay was seldom more than momentary: "Don't suppose you told your 'guy' the full story of our evening together in Vancouver, did you?"

"That's our little secret. You've nothing to worry about on that score."

"You mean I've another reason for concern?"

"Well, it's sort of the old joke about there's good news and there's bad . . . actually it's one reason I called you in the first place."

"What's up?"

"Your willy, that's what!" Charles could imagine a smile breaking out on her face.

"What in hell do you mean?"

"Let me put it this way," she said. "Have you noticed any swelling or tenderness in your penis? I don't mean . . . that kind of swelling."

"No," he replied, certain of his statement, but still wondering if it was a joke of some kind.

"They say that fifty per cent of men show no symptoms at all."

"Pardon me?"

"I hate to admit this to you, but I've got a case of *chlamydia*—just diagnosed—and since there's a chance I had it when we were together in Vancouver, I felt I had to let you know. You better get yourself along to the family doctor for an antibiotic. That'll clear it up."

Charles knew Joan was not joking. He fell silent for a long time and then he said, "It seems I am now doubly in your debt." Afterwards, his words struck him as awkward, but the sincerity was genuine. It was time now to cover all bases. "Belated thanks," he said, "for putting in a favourable word for me. Thanks, too, for letting me know there was . . . well . . . an unexpected sting in the tail, so to speak, of our night together. I won't forget what you've done for me."

"I'll take that in a positive sense," Joan said, satisfied now with fulfilling the original purpose of her call. "If you want to see me again, I'd love it. No obligation, Charles. None. I'm a big girl. Realistic, too. I don't expect much from the married guys. But damn you all, you're a hell of a lot better than the unmarried dorks I meet most of the time. Take care." With that, she hung up before he could reply.

Not that Charles had anything significant to say at this point. What could he say? He sat a bit stunned for a moment, the receiver still in his hand. Then he reached for his address book and phoned his doctor's office for an appointment.

Good news and bad news, he reflected on, as he waited for the receptionist's answer. Not many women would have had the guts—and the consideration—to do what Joan had just done. He would remember that part of their recent adventure fondly. Now he had to get to Brisson's documents.

CHAPTER 3

1

For the most part, the file relating to the Washington trip was unexceptional. As André Brisson had said, the photocopies of hotel bills, car rentals, plane tickets and miscellaneous expenses all appeared to be in order. The purpose of the trip, according to an expense form, was a seminar sponsored by the Washington-based Urban Institute—a think tank specializing in objective, serious research on urban government and services.

Charles concocted an explanation for Dan's Washington trip. (He acknowledged—to himself solely, and then only in his most truthful moments—that he was wrong as often as he was right in wild guesses of this kind. However, he was addicted to the venerable tradition of the "reporter's hunch" and could do nothing to control it.) Dan must have been assigned the file on reinventing a federal role in urban affairs, and it seemed perfectly logical that Dan would've attended the conference to pick the brains of some of the best urban policy analysts the U.S. had to offer.

Attached to the list of expenses were receipts for a registration fee and a gala dinner on the Saturday evening, and another for an oyster brunch at the Maryland Golf and Country Club on the Sunday. A rental car was checked in at the Washington airport at 2:45 p.m.; a ticket for the Ottawa airport parking lot was stamped 5:35 p.m. The airline ticket—showing a return flight from Washington to Ottawa direct, leaving 9:10 p.m. and arriving 10:45 p.m.—was hardly incriminating. It would have been like Dan— assuming it was Dan—to have taken a chance on an earlier flight to arrive home a few hours ahead of his original schedule. Considering the poor guy had given up his weekend for his job, Charles allowed, you could hardly blame him for that.

The Barbados documents were more interesting. Charles had to admit that the details did not add up, mainly because many pieces to the puzzle appeared to be missing. There were enough, however, to capture his attention.

For starters, the purpose of the gathering was not evident. The Canadian High Commission picked up the full tab for the food and accommodation for the resort weekend. From the room assignment memo, thoughtfully stapled to the hotel bill by one of the Canadian high commissioner's staff, it looked like a meeting of senior officials from a cross-section of the Organization of American States.

Mexico was not there, nor was Colombia or Ecuador. Nevertheless, other members including Argentina, Panama, Venezuela, Peru and the United States were involved, along with a number of Caribbean states like Trinidad and Tobago. What the Canadian High Commission in Barbados had to do with the meeting was not evident—other than a vague suggestion that it handled logistics and served as formal sponsor of the event.

Grounds for inclusion of participants were certainly not obvious in the credentials of the majority of participants. Panama sent the Director of Airport Safety and Security and a vice-president of the state-controlled National Post Office and Telecommunications Corporation. Argentina offered a high-ranking official of the Department of Agriculture and another from the Ministry of the Interior responsible for national security. The Associate Director, Drug Enforcement Agency, an assistant to the White House Chief of Staff, and a covey of minor officials represented the United States.

The Canadian participants were Chief Inspector Mike Burnham, head of the RCMP detachment in Vancouver, and Dan Carpenter, described as Director International Projects. The notion that Dan was present at such a meeting was more implausible than his title.

Considering that the sole basis for suspecting Carpenter's involvement was the room assignment memo, Charles was inclined to think that the mystery participant was not actually Dan; rather, someone whose involvement authorities had wanted for some unknown reason to conceal. Except for two further observations, Charles would have passed the file back to Brisson at this point and reported a dead end.

A pencilled notation against RCMP Inspector Burnham's name caught his eye. Sharply visible in the high-quality photocopy from the original file was the entry "not attending." More significant was the name—Jorge Ramillo-Portes—shown in the room assignment as assistant to Argentina's Secretary General for National Security.

Ramillo-Portes, Charles clearly remembered, had attended a briefing at Industry Canada a few years ago. It was some time after the Free Trade Agreement, and Canada was still at pains to explain its interpretation of the sections relating to defence production to its American neighbours. At that time, Ramillo-Portes was working as a consultant for Multiplex-Contor, an international armaments firm with offices in the United States, Central America and South America. Charles would bet the farm on this, because it came up several times in the conversation the two of them had with Dan Carpenter over drinks at the end of the session.

At the reception, Ramillo-Portes had pontificated at length on the "hypocrisy" of official U.S. policy on arms sales to Third World countries, claiming that U.S. firms could enjoy unrestricted commerce, providing only that the regimes in question were those favoured by the American administration. The Mexican, or Colombian, or Argentinean—he never did say which country he called home—seemed to warm to the give and take of the discussion, especially after Dan joined in. Charles had withdrawn from it after the hyperbolic conversation got too much for him to take. However, to this day, he could recall the scene as he left the room: Ramillo-Portes and Dan enjoying each other's company, arms gesticulating wildly, trading drink for drink at the bar, oblivious to the looks of the servers and barmen keen to finish up and go home.

Charles tallied his conclusions from his first reading of the AG's file. Dan—if in fact it was Dan—was at a meeting in Barbados, at the same time he was apparently attending an event in Washington. Dan was also previously acquainted with at least one of the attendees, whose presence seemed no more explicable. The gathering was a ragbag of international representatives, one of which was a former arms industry consultant, now freshly minted as an Argentinean government official. Many participants seemed to have some connection with police work or maybe anti-terrorism, but it was hardly a label that fitted everyone.

Charles felt a thrill run up and down his backbone. More like the stimulant of the investigative journalist's recognition of a hot lead, than the deeper, calming feeling of satisfaction the public servant enjoys from a job well done. It was a level of exhilaration that had been missing in his life for a long time.

The AG's file, Charles had to admit, was more ambiguous than he had supposed. The job called for some real effort—that he could plainly see. He was convinced, as well, that his best approach, given his main objective of getting the Auditor General off his back—and Dan's—was to act without further delay. He'd have to make up for the days lost to inaction, if he was to accommodate Brisson's deadline with his boss. He would *imply* commitment to the task by giving Brisson his damned report not later than Monday afternoon and be done with it. Of course, in that case he would have to do some real sniffing around. Try to add any kind of new element to Dan's case based on something concrete that he found. Fine. Report immediately. Where should he start? On what? Nothing obvious leapt to mind.

The more he considered his predicament, the more he paced his office floor, the more Charles realized that he knew nothing about the current life of Mr. Dan Carpenter. Though they worked in the same office building, and for the same boss, it finally struck him that Dan seemed never to be in the neighbourhood. Secretaries mentioned his name in hushed tones, adding to the mystery of his absence, but the plain fact was the guy was virtually invisible. Brisson had suggested paying attention to Dan's "habits." How was he to do this, when he wasn't there to observe?

When he wasn't there to observe. This thought repeated itself in Charles's imagination until it resolved into his first substantial idea since he took to pacing. He rifled through the Montebello file on the corner of his desk. Confirmed. Not brilliant. But at least a start. He called in his secretary. She would have an important phone call to make on his behalf before she could start her weekend.

2

Dan's drive to Montebello during the late autumn afternoon was a joy—as it normally is on weekdays when there is only local traffic. Once past Thurso and the stinking sulphur fumes spewing from its paper mills, the old highway hugged the scenic eastern shore of the vast Ottawa River.

Dotted in winter with ice-fishing shacks, the shallow bays and marshes on that day were the hiding place of hunters starting to gather in the dimming light in time for the evening landing flights of Canada geese and rich varieties of ducks. Tall poplars on the distant islands—their tips caught by the setting sun—stood like bronzed arrowheads against the dark clouds lining the horizon.

The river, stretched to its limit in the widest parts, now gave no hint of the turbulence a few miles upstream. Its icy shimmer—majestic and tranquil at the same time—drew the driver into a reflective mood.

Dan could not reconstruct precisely when the line was crossed. It did not happen in the first years after he joined the federal government; but it did not take long, either. Some might say Dan simply coveted the rich and wanted to get as much of the good life as he could grasp. An independent observer with a flair for amateur psychology, he believed, might put it all down to an early tendency to escapism.

Raised in a strict Baptist home, ruled by a relentlessly demanding mother, Dan soon learned to "measure up" within the home to the high standards of behaviour and expression imposed by the Carpenter family code. Youngest of three—his two sisters were three and seven years older—Dan found almost no time for himself. Homework, piano lessons, church and Sunday school, followed by afternoon car rides for a family treat. Only the regular Saturday afternoon ball game in the local park gave a break from the dull routine.

It wasn't merely the ball game Dan enjoyed. What meant most was the chance to mix with friends. To stretch out on the grass after the game, listen to dirty jokes, hear stories of sexual adventures that the others always seemed to enjoy. To get a peek, in truth, at a world the Carpenters had done their best to wall off from their son.

With time, tales of his friends' youthful exploits lost some of their allure. Like the blow job Bobby Tupper got from Susan Martin, while standing on a toilet seat in the girls' washroom. Or the time, as legend had it, Bobby was raped by two country girls who confined him to the back seat of a car and "fucked his ass off" for a whole day. While Dan heard dozens of wild ones like that, he couldn't tell a joke, let alone contribute a real-life experience.

Dan never shed his fascination with the Bobby Tuppers of this world or their lifestyles. Progressively, his taste for the company of exotics (his word) deepened. Indeed, by the time he returned home for the Christmas holidays after his first term at McGill University, Dan had collected a stable of casual acquaintances—drug pushers, pimps, and the odd small-time loan enforcer—whose company he had sought out in the sleazy watering holes of lower rue Ste-Catherine in Montreal. At this point, Dan remembered, he had no desire to copy what they did; his pleasure came from simply hanging around them. Maybe, he reflected, he would never have become involved so deeply if . . .

Wherever this memory was going, it froze in mid-air, as soon as Dan saw the lights of the resort hotel on his right. Downshifting his BMW, he turned up the long driveway.

Inside, he could see Roger Lavigne and Francine Coté completing registration. Different floors, not separate beds, he thought to himself, giving expression to the suspicion he had harboured for some time. It was a viewpoint—this one with no foundation in reality—that fitted Dan's outlook on most of the world around him.

To his two colleagues Dan spoke without a trace of innuendo: "*Bonsoir Roger. Bonsoir Francine. J'espère que le voyage était agréable.*" Then switching to English to reflect a more spontaneous informality: "Don't wait for me. I'll catch up in a minute. I suppose the others are at the bar. So I'll join you there as soon as I've registered."

"Fred and Norm got here early," Lavigne said. "We're going to join them at the bar right now. However, Charles Haversham will miss our meeting. His secretary called to say that his wife is out of town and their daughter came down suddenly with a nasty virus. He has had to stay home this weekend to look after her."

CHAPTER 4

1

Except for a few tourists hustling off to the Byward Market, Elgin Street was a virtual wasteland, as Charles hurried towards his office early Saturday morning. The wind was chilling, leaving no doubt that winter would arrive early again this year.

Once committed to dealing promptly with Brisson's request, Charles felt that the Montebello meeting presented an opportunity he could not miss. He had considered the idea of attending the getaway to watch Dan at close quarters. However, to his way of thinking, this made better sense as a strategy *after* he had something—anything—concrete to build on. First, he reasoned, he needed to get a better feel for Dan's work in the PCO. One way of doing it was to have a careful look around his office. Moreover, he had more prospects of doing that without arousing suspicion once Dan was off at the retreat.

The excuse of the sick daughter came to Charles without effort. His wife, Diane, was in fact out of town, their daughter, Linda, accompanying her. There was almost no chance of a miscue arising on that front. A Saturday morning visit to the office was also explainable. If encountered by a co-worker, Charles would say he was picking up work for home in the likely event he'd have to take off Monday to care for his ailing patient. His final touch: to ask his secretary to wait until late Friday afternoon to convey to Lavigne's office his excuse for not attending. No need for personal explanations; no chance for Lavigne to insist on his attendance.

The only detail that concerned him now was the compulsory signing-in and signing-out at security, and the length of time required to make the most of the visit. Twenty minutes seemed right. Anything longer would look strange to anyone paying attention, considering the alibi he intended to use.

Although he had formulated a scheme to investigate Dan's office, Charles had no clear picture of what useful starting point he could expect to find there. His lack of clarity reflected his ambivalent reaction to the current mission. If Dan was involved in something offbeat, Charles thought, he was unlikely to leave evidence of it sitting around on his desk. Dan's padlocked security cabinet, for which only Dan and his secretary had the combination, could not be a source of clues. No secrets from the computer either, entry being barred by an individual password requirement, which Dan, like all his colleagues, kept from others.

His best hope, it seemed, was to gain entry to Dan's desk. All confidential files would be locked away, but Dan's agenda book would probably be there. It would help him to reconstruct the pattern of Dan's meetings and travel. Carbon copies of Dan's expense forms might also be stuck somewhere in the desk. His messages and telephone chits were worth a look-see, too, although Charles began to question—his distaste for snooping on a friend mounting—whether this effort was likely to prove rewarding. Charles needed a coffee, a moment to rethink everything. Tim Hortons to the rescue.

2

It was an old Coca-Cola slogan, Charles recalled, as he resumed his route: "The pause that refreshes." It wasn't one of Tim Hortons' mottos, but the effect of the stop at the coffee shop had spurred his determination to get on with it, nonetheless.

Once seated with a comforting warm brew, Charles had worked himself back to action by what now appealed to him as a fully convincing route. Perhaps his half-drunken haze had obscured the point at the time; a principal in the Office of the Auditor General does not call every day suggesting private sleuthing in a public cause. It was an unusual step, Charles fully recognized, one implying that Brisson—no doubt after the most careful analysis— had concluded that exceptional circumstances dictated exceptional action. Like it or not, he had to take Brisson seriously.

Perhaps the real target was not Dan Carpenter himself. That would make it easier. Hadn't Brisson said something about investigating others? Did he mean in the Privy Council Office? Or elsewhere? The file must be far from routine.

As the ambivalence faded, Charles decided that if he were to play the detective's role for a while, he would do it as professionally as possible. He'd make the most of his visit and examine thoroughly everything he could lay his hands on. As he entered his office building, Charles found himself looking on his modest adventure in a much more positive light.

"Good morning, sir," said the commissionaire seated at the entrance by the elevator. Charles scribbled his name, date, room number and time in a black book lying on a desk.

The guard looked up from his newspaper. "What floor?"

"Eleventh."

"May I see your pass?"

Damn.

"Well this is the first time . . . left it at home . . . I only need to go to my office for a few minutes." Charles was not sure if he was angry at his inattention to detail or his present grovelling.

The little man with the big hat and the emblem proudly displayed on his shoulder looked unimpressed.

"Can't you make an exception?" Charles asked. "Let me sign in and you can verify it on Monday."

"I'm sorry, but Mr. Harris has left strict instructions—"

"Who? You mean *Fred* Harris, the director of economic planning? What the hell's he doing . . . ?"

After a pause and a deep breath: "Look. Mr. Harris and I work together on the same floor. He's a friend of mine. You need have no concern that you're doing a small favour for me in a good cause. I need to get into my office."

"*Sais pas,*" the guard said, staring at his feet. "I don't know if—"

"Why don't you simply look the other way? See, here's my elevator access card for God's sake. Let me use it now and I'll be back down before you know it."

Slowly the security officer edged away from the elevator door. Charles swiped his access card before the officer could change his mind.

After such a rocky start, Charles was relieved not to be met by others on the floors between or greeted at the eleventh when the doors slid open. Better than anticipated, none of his colleagues had come to the office that morning. No reason to think some workaholic wouldn't show up at some time on the weekend. For now, however, the floor was his. Finally, good luck was running his way.

Charles went directly to his computer, logged on, and set a print task for the draft report prepared Friday by his assistant. He would get it later from the high-speed printer in the administrative services room up the hall.

Leaving his office door ajar, he went straight to the men's washroom, stopped briefly to check inside and slapped a large "Out of Order" sign on the door. He had knocked it off on his home computer before leaving. Charles mouthed a silent "Yes!" Getting into the spirit of the thing now. Then he continued to the end of the hall and turned the corner. Picking up his pace, he glanced left and right as he rushed down the hall, trying to assure himself of a clear fix on the location of the women's washroom.

Charles opened Dan's door using his office master key. He was now irretrievably committed. How long could he count on the security guard sitting tight? What if the little toad decided to check the floor? Reluctantly, Charles restricted his stay to ten minutes, still enough for a systematic search of Dan Carpenter's office.

The layout was as expected, perhaps a touch more Spartan than his own. Dan's empty desktop and orderly credenza conveyed the image of an uncluttered mind and careful organizer—exemplary graduate of Time Management Inc. that Dan was.

The open desk was a pleasant surprise. As he rifled through the contents of the upper drawer, he was gratified he had not had to force the desk lock, considering the meagre reward. No agenda book. No copies of expense forms, either. Mostly memos relating to the time of meetings or newspaper clippings—organized around no topic in particular. The bottom drawer proved much the same. He could hardly be disappointed, given his modest expectations. Still, he found himself hoping he would find something confirmatory— anything he could use to make his effort seem convincing to Brisson.

One inference came from what he did *not* see. Nothing in the clippings, the references to meetings with other departmental officials, or the photocopies of journal articles showed any evidence that Dan was working on the revival of a federal role in city politics, as Charles had thought. In fact, to judge from Dan's themeless files and the computer games lying in the top drawer, he did not appear to be working on much of anything. Charles examined every piece of paper anyway, determined not to overlook the slightest detail. With waning enthusiasm, he turned to the top right-hand drawer, where he stored his pencils, pens and paper clips; he expected Dan to do the same.

The drawer was nearly empty, making it easy, at least, to review its contents. Charles took care in examining each item: a current Air Canada schedule, two ballpoint pens, an inexpensive Sharp calculator (one without sufficient functions for even relatively simple statistical calculations), a package of yellow Post-it notes, and a nearly full box of Privy Council Office business cards. He pulled a card from the box, hoping it would offer a better clue to what Dan was doing than the files he had just examined.

The card took Charles no further along that road. As he had seen in PCO memos, Dan was described as "Adviser, Major Projects"—a job title as grand and uninformative as his own. Charles twirled the card gently in his fingers, reflecting for a few seconds on the futility of the morning's activities. With a deep sigh, he fitted the business card back into the pack.

It was then Charles noticed what he had missed earlier. A few cards in the middle of the stack had evidently been removed before, and in the process had become a little greyed. Like a thin line of chocolate icing between two layers of a vanilla cake, these business cards stood out against the pristine whiteness of the others.

Charles took great care with his next move. After picking out all of the previously handled cards, he set them out on the desk—from left to right—in the order he had taken them from the box. A glance was all he needed to confirm they were indeed Dan's business cards, exactly like the rest.

He turned the first card over.

Written with evident precision on the back was the following mishmash:

^81@@&(Ld

The detail on the back of the other cards was not so complex, though no less puzzling:

7890 9811 0022 4598

574 889 8654

JRPDEC2

574 887 7204

Charles had no idea what any of the numbers meant and, were it not for their location, would probably have paid little attention to any of them. However, his curiosity had been aroused by the manner in which they'd been hidden. As he continued to stare at the numbers, letters and symbols, the ex-reporter in him became more intrigued. Although he could not imagine how any of this tied in with the AG's concerns, it was obvious to him that they must have some real significance. The information on these cards, he convinced himself, was important—important, at least, to Dan.

Charles recorded on a slip of paper what he found written on the back of each card, assigning a number to reflect their position in the box. He might as well be meticulous with his one fascinating discovery and take away some kind of record, however unclear the meaning. The rest of his office search had hardly been worth the effort.

He returned Dan's cards to the centre of the pack, rearranged the card box, pens and Post-its as he found them, and closed the desk. Retracing his steps, he surveyed the empty hall, closed Dan's office door, and picked up his printout in the administration office.

Remembering to remove the sign from the men's washroom as he passed, Charles allowed himself the luxury of a satisfied smile. Home free. No interference from security. No damage to anything in Dan's office. And, thank God, no need to use that lame excuse about the men's washroom being out of order to explain his presence in another corridor. His first reaction was to think he would have been unconvincing in that lie.

Why be so negative? Although the day may not have produced results he could pass on to the AG, the plan had gone well. Well enough, considering the temporary foul-up with the security pass, to treat himself to a fine sushi lunch.

CHAPTER 5

1

With wife and daughter away for the weekend, Charles had the run of the house. He loaded his CD player with the best of his seventies music, selected the shuffle-play option, and cranked up the volume to what his wife, Diane, would have considered an intolerable level. Then he wandered to the den and buried himself in his comfortable easy chair. He had forgotten what it was like to enjoy a Saturday afternoon at home, free of marital bickering.

Charles had come to second-guess more frequently his earlier unwillingness to seize the openings Diane had offered him with her repeated threats of divorce. He often daydreamed now of one final confrontation. Earlier, he was not yet prepared for such dramatic action. Then he had preferred to stall, to find some kind of compromise solution in the interest of a measure of domestic stability. Charles had rationalized his tolerance of domestic discontentment in terms of the worse effects of the alternative. He could put up with her annoying ways, he used to think, so long as it did not interfere with the pursuit of his career in the public service.

Charles had also been sympathetic to the case his wife had constructed as the wronged party in their relationship. Although he had vigorously denied that his career was not progressing well in Ottawa, and had been in no mood to take responsibility for Diane's unrealistic aspirations, he did recognize that his wife was the clear loser in the relocation from Toronto to Ottawa. He had seen that she would have to get back into publishing somehow—even if it meant commuting, even if it meant having to pay for a housekeeper/ nanny during the week. The idea had appeared to be a simple solution, and Charles had pressed it successfully, using all the persuasive power he could muster.

For a while, the new arrangement had seemed a substantial improvement. The intellectual stimulation of Diane's editorial assignments drove out her earlier boredom; the inconveniences of the workweek exacted a small price, but roughly equally from both parties. Weekends appeared better than either could remember since their early courtship days—stimulating conversation, the occasional pleasant dinner party with friends, an elevated level of social activity in general—simply because everything they did together was compressed. For a few years, Charles's marriage fix—as Diane had described it to friends on her more upbeat days—appeared as a workable accommodation to the needs of both partners.

Eventually, the strain of commuting and the consequences of spending more time apart than together had cancelled the benefits. The old anger in Diane's reaction to events had disappeared— Charles had taken away the grounds for resentment. In its place had grown disconnectedness, an indifference to each other that was reinforced by the awkward hours of seemingly unending weekends. In time, their experiment in reviving a never robust marriage had collapsed under the weight of strains sufficient to test the best of marriages.

By mutual agreement, Diane had given up her job with Maclean Hunter. It was a decision she could not have imagined making earlier, but she began to see signs daily of the toll that extra pressure had exerted on her work. If she could not perform at her peak, she would do something else. At thirty-nine-and-a-half years of age, she would throw herself into the role of housekeeper in their "tiny" Patterson Avenue bungalow; she would spend more time with her daughter; she would take up gardening; she might even try volunteer work in the community. And she would get smashed whenever the consequences of her new avocation became oppressive. From where Charles sat, the transition had, on balance, been a failure. More often than not, the booze had won.

As long as Diane had worked at Maclean Hunter, the den, in which Charles now luxuriated, had been her private reserve. After her resignation, she rapidly lost all interest in the comfortable workspace she had created. Within a few weeks, Charles had taken over the den as his own refuge; within a few months, he had transformed it from a gracefully decorated, stylish home office into something resembling a cross between a museum and a storage room.

For Charles, what was principally lacking in his newly acquired territory were shelves, a deficiency that he had set about to correct with a fanatic's zeal. Notoriously incompetent as a carpenter, he had solved the problem with second-hand bookshelves—four huge oak things, each weighing half a ton—that he had found one Saturday morning at a garage sale. Diane had said the place looked like a "bloody barricade." A more charitable critic might have found that the den still had some of the charm endowed by its previous tenant, if Charles had been content to use bookshelves exclusively for books. This was not to be.

Charles had reserved each shelving unit for a specific interest. At least in his original plan. Things had not quite worked out that way with the unit nearest the door, which so far looked like a kind of sorting area. Magazines, pages torn from newspapers, theatre playbills, travel flyers, golf scorecards, and an assortment of personal bills accumulated in an erratic pile, their precise location and significance known only to the Den Master. On the two bottom shelves lay stacks of unread newspapers, growing mustier with each passing day, their import unknown even to Charles.

On the long wall of the den, two units stood side by side. If he had scrapped one of them, he might have displayed his photographs perfectly well on the wall. Again, that was not Charles's way. When he had been a university student living at home, he'd mounted many of his most treasured photos in stand-up frames. He had displayed them that way before he was married, and he displayed them that way again in his new den. Today they stood carefully arranged on the upper shelves of one bookcase, spaced to provide an unobstructed view of each subject.

The photos had languished for years in boxes, stuck away in storage areas of apartments too small to accommodate an exhibition of his early artistic talent. Now, they were liberated, vivid reminders of the rugged land and boiling rivers he had canoed through with his family in his youth.

Charles could not decide whether to use the third bookshelf to store his classical CDs or to house a collection of pocket books he had accumulated over the years. Though his taste in music ran the gamut of centuries and instruments, Charles was not what you would call an eclectic reader. When he found a writer he liked—take William Johnstone, with his more than twenty-five books in the Ashes Series, or Louis L'Amour, or another prolific western writer like Larry McMurtry—Charles would need to buy everything he could get his hands on. Depth, but not much range, you might say.

On the shelf unit nearest his desk, Charles proudly displayed his hockey trophies, neatly organized from his early days in peewee through bantam. In a prominent place on the top shelf was a framed photo of the University of Western Ontario hockey team that managed to get to the semi-finals in 1974, when Charles—Chuck then to his teammates—played left wing on the third line. Suited in shoulder pads, he appeared even bigger than his six-foot-one frame.

Whenever he looked at the photograph, Charles felt good about himself. Since graduation from his hometown university—more precisely, since he first went to Ottawa as a journalist in the parliamentary press corps—he had become something of a loner. He was glad to have had the comradeship of sport when he was younger; he sometimes wished he had more of it now, as he entered middle age.

As he sat in his den, listening to Chicago, he found himself drawn back to the results of his perusal of Dan's office that morning. Judged against his marching orders, the secret inspection had been a bust. He had discovered nothing that cast light on the AG's examination of unreported travel expenses. Correct that. The absence of work-related materials made it seem improbable that Dan was engaged in business travel of any kind. Charles acknowledged that the AG's documentation contradicted that conclusion. However you sliced it, though, it came to the same thing. He had nothing he could tell Brisson that bore on Dan's mysterious travel.

On the other hand, ever since leaving the office building, Charles had been preoccupied with a question he felt compelled to try to answer—for his own sake. What was the significance of the numbers on those cards? Why would Dan spirit them away as he did, then not bother to lock the desk? Was there some common theme to the numbers, letters and symbols? He craved answers to these questions to satisfy his own curiosity. Perhaps it would help to see the letters and numbers again as he had found them in Dan's desk.

Charles took out the scrap of paper he had used that morning and transferred each set of figures to a separate card. Now he could look for a pattern and observe individual detail.

His eyes settled first on JRPDEC2. Maybe DEC2 meant December 2. If it did, it might be the date of some important event. Was it the date of something yet to come? Or a date from the past? Truth to tell, Charles couldn't be sure of much at this point.

The fact it was written on the back of Dan's personal PCO business card seemed to set one limit to the date reference: Dan joined PCO about a year and a half ago—roughly midway through the year, Charles was quite certain. The balance of probability, he reasoned, was that DEC2 referred to something happening after May, or possibly June, of that year. Okay. But did DEC2 refer to last

December? Or was it December 2 of this year—a little more than a month from now? Anybody's guess.

Don't guess. Think.

Charles took aim at the earlier date. Was last December 2 by any chance the day Dan was supposed to be in Washington and Barbados at the same time? A twinge of excitement again; no need to wonder for long on this one. Verification lay right there in his briefcase.

Charles flipped through Brisson's file in search of the critical document. He was sure the Canadian High Commission's documents contained the information he needed. A moment's effort proved he was right—to a point—but the documentation did not fully confirm the essence of his hunch. The meeting records showed the Barbados gathering was in December. But not on the second. The weekend in question had fallen on December 7 and 8.

Still, Charles hated to give up. Did DEC2 refer to a meeting *before* the Washington–Barbados events? Charles pounded the desk with his fist. Assuming any kind of link to the Barbados meeting was sheer speculation and he knew it.

Discovering the possible significance of a future date—on the assumption that DEC2 referred to the coming month of December— seemed even more of a reach. Charles began to think that the date hypothesis could be completely wrong. The "JRP" part of the thing could not refer to a month—was obviously not a date. So why did he think DEC2 was a date? Had he jumped too readily to the most obvious explanation? He liked the simplicity of his original intuition; it was getting harder to maintain his enthusiasm.

The ring of the telephone broke this train of thought.

"Hello, Daddy," a small voice said. "I miss you." It was his daughter on the line. A few inches shorter than her classmates, Linda more than made up for first impressions of a younger appearance with a manner that was strikingly mature. Cheerful, optimistic, and scrupulously neat in appearance, she presented such a stark contrast with her mother that those who did not know better assumed she must be adopted. Linda remained oblivious to the unfavourable comparison: she loved her mother with an intensity not unusual in the attraction of opposites.

"Well, I miss you too, Sweetie. Are you having fun at Grandma's?"

"I'm not at Grandma's, Daddy. Mommy and I are in Montreal with Auntie Beth. We're staying in a, like, big hotel."

"Oh."

"We went shopping this morning in these really cool little stores in this old part—"

"May I speak with your mother?"

"Mommy isn't here now. She said she'd be in Auntie Beth's room for a few minutes, and then she'd be right back, that's why I called you. I was, like, starting to get lonely."

Charles was both irritated with Diane and touched that Linda had thought to call him in her tiny moment of distress. As the gap between husband and wife had widened over recent years, he had noted to his chagrin that the relationship between mother and daughter had grown closer. Charles, feeling squeezed out in the process, suspected that Diane was using Linda as a pawn in their marriage game. Fresh salt for old wounds. Despite his struggle to find a way to right the balance, to convey genuine, uncalculated affection towards their only child, he felt he had never fully connected. Could it be her present call proved he had done better than he feared? Certainly, he had no wish now to spoil whatever progress he had made and drag a ten-year-old girl into exposing further the curious behaviour of her mother.

"Mommy'll be back in a few minutes, I'm sure," he consoled. "Don't worry. But you be sure to call me again, if she's not back in half an hour."

"Okay, Daddy. 'Bye."

Charles had something new to reflect on. The effort to make sense of his colleague's mysterious cards was now secondary to his puzzlement over what had just transpired. Admittedly, it was not unheard of for him to ignore the details of his wife's social agenda, content that whatever it was she was planning represented a respite from their domestic turmoil. However, he thought he had heard this one right: she had said they were going late afternoon on Friday to Brockville. At least he was now quite sure that is what Diane had said.

What difference did it make that she had taken their daughter and her sister to Montreal instead of visiting her parents? Only the surprise factor, he supposed. He was now satisfied, after a moment of sober consideration, that Linda would get more out of a trip to Montreal than a stifling weekend with doting seniors. Charles decided not to mention the subject, if Diane failed to bring it up. *Show some consistency, man. Don't play the control freak now, when most of the time you don't care what she does.*

By the time Charles got back to the cards, he was nearly convinced that Diane *had* mentioned a shopping trip with Beth. Or was it only with Linda? It didn't seem to matter now. He was into the meaning of the five cards again. The JRPDEC2 card continued to intrigue him.

"Now start over again," Charles said aloud, as if by speaking he could reinforce his powers of concentration. It appeared to work, as he enjoyed a fresh burst of inspiration.

What if JRPDEC2 is a compression of the initials of someone Dan was to meet and the date of a meeting?

You don't know it was a meeting. Or a date.

Look at the JRP. You're working on a person's initials.

Right.

Now, whose initials?

Not a clue.

And DEC?

A long pause, and then Charles yelled at the top of his voice: "Damn! Not a date at all!"

Those initials belong to Dan Carpenter.

He would need to check staff résumés in the office files to confirm the middle initial; it would be useful to see, at the same time, if anything located there helped with JRP. He was in no mood, however, to push his luck with office security a second time that day. Charles was going to have to wait until Monday morning to verify his hunch.

Pleased as he was with his modest breakthrough, Charles knew he was nowhere in his search for an explanation of the other cards. He had a few ideas on a couple of the numbers, not enough though to get excited about. What he needed at this stage was a mind less encumbered by knowledge of the situation—partial as his own was—and the personality of the major character in the piece. Charles required a more objective perspective on his conundrum.

He thought immediately of Mark Gilmore, a former colleague at the *Toronto Star*. Mark was now working in Ottawa as a stringer for a chain of U.S. newspapers. Though they saw each other infrequently, the two men kept in touch, attending an occasional Ottawa Senators' hockey game or having a beer together after work. Mark, Charles always felt, could have been anything he wanted to be. A whiz at computers, a fine raconteur, a brilliant bridge player (never satisfied with his partner), Mark could have flourished in either development or sales within Ottawa's rapidly expanding high tech world.

Mark, however, saw himself as a newspaperman. It was his first job, and—as he often said—if his work was good enough for his editors, it was good enough for him. Charles had called on Mark for advice in the past and had always found two qualities he badly needed now: encyclopaedic knowledge and complete trustworthiness. *Well worth a call.*

Mark could see him early that evening. Charles was impatient. To his great relief, Mark agreed when Charles invited himself to a before-dinner drink.

2

After a sip of single malt, Charles came to the purpose of his visit. He took the five cards from his pocket and invited Mark to move closer.

"I'm not going to give you background on this, Mark," Charles explained. "I'm going to ask you to look at five sets of numbers, letters and symbols, and tell me what you think they represent. The only clue I'll give you is that these numbers were on cards, hidden in a person's desk."

"Is there a prize for the right answer?" Mark asked with a grin.

"No prize, because I don't have the answers myself. That's why I'm here."

"Simply wondering," Mark said, his face now taking on Charles's serious expression.

Charles set out each card on the table. "I don't know whether there is any real significance to their order, but this is how I found them."

Card 1 ^81@@&(Ld

Card 2 7890 9811 0022 4598

Card 3 574 889 8654

Card 4 JRPDEC2

Card 5 574 887 7204

"Now, right off the top, what do you think they could mean?"

Mark studied the overall pattern and looked carefully at each card in turn before speaking. "It's impossible to be sure whether some of these numbers belong in pairs or stand alone. I'd bet you, though, card two is a banking-related number—could be a Visa or MasterCard number . . . or maybe a bank card number."

"You think?"

"I'm sure it's tied to an account of some kind. Possibly it's a bank card number to get into an online account. If 7890 etc. *is* linked to an Internet account, whoever owns it could be using it, along with a password, to access the account and pay bills, using a computer."

"Any thoughts on the password?"

"Maybe card one . . . card four looks a better bet, though."

"Can you tell what bank it is?"

"Not from the numbers. But there are only a few offering online banking. You don't need the branch, just the bank itself—assuming, of course, I'm not totally full of it on this line of speculation."

"Well, park that idea . . . for the moment," Charles said, a broad smile filling his face. "What else do you see?"

Mark picked up two cards and set them off to one side. "Cards three and five look for all the world like phone numbers," he said. "Judging from the way the numbers have been grouped, I'm sure the first set of three numbers is an area code and the rest of it's the phone number."

"I'm inclined to agree with you," Charles said, pleased to have confirmation of his first hunch. "They might be telephone numbers—but do you suppose it's that straightforward? Maybe the digits are jumbled."

Mark had an immediate opinion on this one. "If someone has to record a number in the first place," he said, "I think we can assume it is not used often. If that's the case, whoever has had to write it down probably didn't want to get too fancy with any system of encoding—assuming there is some mixing of order going on—or he wouldn't be able to remember how that works either."

"Makes sense to me, now that I hear you say it."

"Also, it looks as if the two telephone numbers are for the same area, since what we're calling the area code is identical and the first three digits of the telephone number itself are virtually the same on the two cards."

"So that suggests no jumbling of numbers, I take it."

"I think one should always look for something simple, at least as a starting assumption. I'd check the three-digit area code part of the number for a start. Then if that doesn't produce anything you think is promising, try mixing the area code numbers and see what gives. If the area code is reversed, that may be a clue to the order of other numbers as well."

"Good. I'll play with that later. Now what do you make of the rest?"

Mark sipped his Scotch. Then he lit a cigar. He said nothing. Charles leaned forward in anticipation of his guru's next divination; there was only silence. Finally Mark spoke. Haltingly, as if in pain, his ego wounded by the admission of partial failure.

"I'm afraid, laddie, that we're left with too many promising possibilities. I'm certainly not prepared to do more than hazard a guess at this point."

"Oh, go on."

Mark appeared less confident than earlier.

Finally, he spoke in a positive tone. "The more I think about it, the more I'm convinced card one is a computer password . . . and four is a user ID . . . or maybe a banking password."

"You said it *is* an online banking password."

"Look, Charles. You can't be definitive on these things. It could be. It could also be a credit card PIN. Who knows? I sure don't."

"Oh." Although disappointed, Charles would not let it show. "Okay," he said, "I'll be more patient."

"Let's break the rest of this down," Mark urged. "Take it one step at a time. Start by comparing card one and card four. What do you conclude?"

"Four's much less complex than card one."

"Right. So what's that suggest?"

"Damn it, Mark, if I knew that I wouldn't be here asking you."

Mark refreshed their glasses. Charles looked sheepish. "It's the relative simplicity of the code on card four," Mark said, choosing his words carefully, "that makes me think it's meant to go along with another set of numbers."

"I see where you're headed now," Charles said. "That's why you think card four might be a banking password . . . and the tricky stuff on card one makes it a stand-alone password to a computer."

"Right. I'd also bet," Mark added after a pause, "the computer password, on card one, is not often used. You'd never want anything as complex as that for your home or office. No. This baby is meant for a remote computer of some kind. One that our mystery person accesses only rarely."

"One hell of a performance, Mr. Holmes!"

"There are still loose ends, my friend."

"I know. But I'm further ahead than when I walked in."

As he got up to leave, Charles made an observation he had struggled to keep to himself. "I didn't want to bias your thinking earlier, Mark. So I didn't say anything. I'm sure I've found at least part of the explanation for card four. I was thrown off for a while by DEC2, thinking it was a date. But now, putting together what you said with what I figured out before, I'm sure it's a password made up of two people's initials. I think I know one, but not the other."

Charles paused for a moment to reconsider the full impact of his exchange with Mark. Some details now made more sense; much remained to explain. Still, he felt his friend had pointed him in useful new directions. Some of them appeared ominous.

"Keep this numbers business under your hat," Charles said. "I'm not sure where all this is headed, but if it's somewhere bad, I may soon need your hat, your brains and your big army boots."

3

Stretched out on his couch at home, Charles found that a combination of drinks had made him forget the "Barbados Caper," as he was now coming to think of it. Mark's smoky single malts, the half-bottle of Ruffino consumed with a pizza picked up on the way home, and now the cognac he was sipping as he watched the crackling logs in the fireplace smoothed out the tensions of the day. Charles felt a warm glow and a powerful urge for sex.

The anticipation of such a possibility had flashed through his mind when he found the excuse to avoid the Montebello meeting. Not merely an excellent opportunity to visit Dan's office, he then concluded. With wife and daughter both away, he also saw the best chance in a while for a good romp. A night of uninhibited pleasure of the kind he had learned to live without at home. No preliminary badgering or manipulation, no post-coital sensitivities or recriminations. Just pure sex.

He rifled through the Yellow Pages, in search of "Escorts."

Charles was well aware that almost every time he was away from home or his wife was away from him, his thoughts seemed to turn to how he could get into bed with a new woman. This reaction had been so much a part of how he had acted for years that the instinct to look for sex usually drove him in that direction whenever he had the opportunity. Such behaviour was to some extent surprising, because whenever Charles went into it deeply, he had to admit that the sex act itself was not paramount for him. The element of uncertainty over how the entire encounter would evolve—rather than its resolution—was what turned him on.

Charles got back to his search for escorts. Something exotic on a chilly fall night would be agreeable. His mind was lost in a review of ads running from the banal to the intriguing. Another sip of cognac; the fumes burned his nose. He let his imagination soar.

He was in a huge brothel, with all the hookers in Ottawa lined up for his inspection and selection. Some wore sunglasses; others wore masks. Tall girls with pointed breasts vied for his attention with shorter ones proudly displaying their silicon enhancements. All in lurid lingerie. He slid slowly past, heady with the potpourri of cheap perfumes exuding from their nearly naked bodies. From time to time, he would stop. The women would put their arms around his neck and press him hard, rubbing seductively into his bare chest. In a flash, Charles narrowed down his choice.

"Asian Beauties" struck his fancy above all else. Dialling rapidly, he hurried through the preliminary shadow boxing, and got down to the essentials of negotiation.

"I want a Thai girl," Charles insisted. "That should be no problem at all," a woman said in a voice that aimed to sound sexy and business-like at the same time. "I have a very nice girl. Twenty-one. Beautiful. How long do you want her to stay?"

The question caught Charles unprepared. His first inclination was to say that if she was as exotic as he was picturing, she could stay forever. However, by the time he came to answer, the fantasy of the preceding moments had vanished and Charles had crashed back to earth. As if the practical details of the impending contract had dashed his mood of adventure.

"Have her call me before she leaves. I expect it will be the normal hour."

CHAPTER 6

1

Less than ten minutes into Monday morning and Charles had satisfied his curiosity over Dan Carpenter's middle initial. His secretary produced a copy of Dan's résumé from the departmental files and the information was confirmed: Daniel Edgar Carpenter, born in Oakville, Ontario. With DEC covered, he could start his search for the owner of the other set of initials. Charles got as far "Putman, William" in the full Privy Council Office staff list, when his phone rang.

"How's your daughter feeling today?" Roger Lavigne inquired, then continued without awaiting a reply. "Too bad you missed Montebello. It was one of our better work sessions. Produced a number of decisions. As a matter of fact, one that affects you in particular. Meet me for lunch today at 12:30—at Hy's—and I'll bring you up to speed on my meeting."

"Looking forward to it."

Charles had concluded, following his session with Mark, that his next step would have to be a conversation with Roger Lavigne. This invitation suited his plans admirably. The numbers found in Dan's office, while intriguing, seemed to have nothing to do directly with Brisson's questions about Dan's curious travel itinerary. If he were going to give anything substantial to Brisson, he would have to get it indirectly from Lavigne.

As for his own interest in Dan Carpenter, Mark's speculation about some kind of banking-related password—now confirmed to be partly made up of Dan's initials—had elevated the mystery, even though no link with the travel expenses issue had been established. Before going further, Charles felt he needed to know what, if anything, Lavigne could bring to the equation. It seemed even more obviously the way to go, now that Lavigne had provided an opening with an invitation to lunch.

2

The two men ordered: Perrier water, cream of asparagus soup, and seafood salad with chili oil and light mayonnaise dressing. Each took a sip of the water. Each sampled the edge of the hot soup. Lavigne was the first to speak.

"It was a productive meeting, but we certainly could have benefited from your input."

"Yes, too bad I wasn't there," Charles said, "especially since something you decided involves me."

"Dan Carpenter, I must say, had a lot to do with that. Put up a most persuasive argument. Said you were the man for the job. But I'm getting ahead of myself," Lavigne said. "Why don't I start at the beginning? You need to have some background. That's the reason, after all, I wanted to get us both out of the office—where we can have a good, uninterrupted chat."

Charles looked intently into Lavigne's face, wondering what he had in store for him. This was, after all, his first lunch with the deputy secretary. In fact, it was the first occasion he'd been one-on-one with his boss since his job interview more than two months earlier. At that time, Charles—who normally felt fully in control of his situation—had struggled to find the right buttons to gain his assessor's confidence.

Charles had been surprised in the first place that he was to be interviewed by a deputy secretary rather than an assistant deputy. However, that was before he learned that Lavigne—who had inherited an assistant deputy secretary responsible for economic development policies when he moved to PCO—had eased out the incumbent and had never seen fit to replace him. Lavigne's "economic policy shop" exhibited what they like to call horizontal structure: everyone of importance reported directly to him.

The candidate had also expected the hiring decision to turn on evidence of his analytical skills, in particular his trenchant criticisms of previous approaches to Team Canada trade missions and the depth of understanding reflected in his solutions. Lavigne, in reality, had been uninterested in the younger man's quick fixes and even less in his diagnoses. Indeed, the deputy secretary appeared uncomfortable whenever Charles's observations on past practice became concrete enough to allow Lavigne to identify specific individuals responsible for the outcomes.

Lavigne's intent in the job interview had been less to probe the substance of the candidate's mind than to convey—by indirection rather than explicit pronouncements—*his* expectations on performance. Smooth interpersonal relations with PCO and PMO staff and officials in other departments, commitment to team play, a capacity always to see the "big picture"—these emerged as the fundamentals of Lavigne's creed. As Charles settled in for the briefing, he recognized from his reflection on their earlier encounter that it might take him a while to read Lavigne's subtext with confidence.

"As you know from the background papers for the meeting," Lavigne said, "the government has to develop a contingency plan for maintaining industrial subsidy arrangements when it's virtually certain the next round of trade talks will make it impossible for Canada to keep most of its research and development support systems, at least in their present form."

"I'm sure Dan had a lot to say on the R&D issue."

"He did. And he would be a logical person to carry the ball on this in the next few months—if we could spare him. Unfortunately, he's on another assignment and I cannot put him full time on the file. That's where we decided you should come in. The PM is against any trade missions in the near future, so you won't be needed there for a while. Instead, we'll put you in the lead on the R&D file, and Dan can serve as backup. He can assume more duties as he's able to shed his current obligation."

Charles saw the door fly wide open. He had not expected it so early, but he was ready. "And what is that obligation? Frankly, I don't have a clear idea of what Dan is up to these days."

Lavigne was silent for what to Charles seemed an eternity. "Well, it's not what it appears."

Charles concealed a sudden intake of air. "How so?" he asked.

The deputy secretary paused again, weighing his response as carefully as if he were briefing the prime minister. "Although it may seem like cloak and dagger drama today," Lavigne replied, as he worked in a few forkfuls of salad, "it was considered serious business at the time."

Charles slid his chair closer to the table and waited for Lavigne to continue. For an instant, he feared that was all he was going to get of Dan's "drama."

"You *are* one of us now," Lavigne said, after giving the matter a great deal of thought. "For this reason I feel I can tell you . . . Dan has been on a highly confidential mission . . . almost from the day he came to PCO."

Glancing around to satisfy himself again that no one could overhear their conversation, Lavigne took a long sip of Perrier. Hesitantly at first, and then with increasing enthusiasm for his subject, Roger Lavigne continued with his absorbing revelations.

"The story begins less than two years ago, when the prime minister and the American president got away for a weekend of golf in Florida. For reasons best known to him, the president had become determined to mount a new version of the War on Drugs. This time, he insisted, there had to be full co-operation from all North and South American governments—at least those he considered trustworthy.

"The co-operative alliance, dubbed the Hemispheric Task Force, was to meet in secret. Mexico and Colombia were excluded completely from the exercise. Every participating country was sworn to abide by an elaborate set of subterfuges. The Americans were determined to prevent the unreliable Mexican and Colombian governments—both shot through with cartel sympathizers, as you know—from learning about the multi-country committee and also, frankly, to avoid the international embarrassment of having to explain Mexico's exclusion from it."

"Fascinating stuff!" Charles said in a manner out of keeping with the seriousness with which Lavigne was recounting his story. *Idiot.*

"The whole idea," Lavigne continued, a disapproving expression still evident on his lined face, "was that a collaborative effort would be made to find more effective means of intercepting drug shipments. One working group would look at water transport, the other air. You may know this, but I'm telling you the American Drug Enforcement Agency has used everything but trained dolphins to try to interrupt movements of drugs, especially cocaine, by boat from Colombia. The Medellin and Cali Cartels in Colombia had frustrated the DEA at every turn and the Americans were desperate to find something to counteract them."

"I've heard about the effectiveness of the drug cartels," Charles said. He was keen to counteract his flippant reaction a few moments earlier, although he was not thrilled with the lame remark he had produced.

"Anyway," Lavigne continued, "the president's staff sold him on the notion of combining satellite observation with flexible deployment of amphibious aircraft. You know, those float planes that we use in firefighting operations. The theory was that more effective shore patrol would disrupt the transfer of drugs from ships to land. With the co-operation of key Caribbean countries and more effective small-scale detection activity, at least divers, rafts, and small powerboats would have a tougher time getting their loads to shore."

"Interesting, but what's this got to do with Dan?"

"I'm coming to that." Lavigne was not impressed with an apparent lack of interest in the broader context he was painting. He began to wonder if it was worth the bother to brief Haversham so thoroughly. After a moment's attention to his lunch, he decided to give him a second chance.

"Although the PM gave the president a verbal commitment right there and then, he had of course to discuss it with members of his cabinet at the first opportunity. I had Fred Harris put together some briefing notes for their meeting—mostly simple stuff, since we didn't have much to go on—setting out among other things the pros and cons of Canadian co-operation in this venture."

A briefing note from Fred Harris. That must have been a beauty.

"Fred couldn't make much of the drug busting aspect of the U.S. idea—he's much too honest for that. He did, however, manage to work in some references to direct economic benefits to Canada from the potential sale of amphibious planes, assuming that this element in the original thinking could be preserved. Several cabinet ministers jumped on the idea and the rest, as they say, is history."

Charles shifted uncomfortably in his chair. "Clever!"

"The plan was to keep close control of Canadian involvement within the Prime Minister's Office and the PCO," Lavigne continued. "We needed someone with industry smarts and at the same time a person whose role would not appear too blatantly obvious. You know very well how it would have gone: the Minister of Industry gets *his* man; so Foreign Affairs would need to have *theirs* and before long we'd have had a whole marching band into the act."

"That sounds like Ottawa to me."

"Well, the secretary to cabinet solved it all with one neat suggestion. We'd transfer in someone with an Industry background for a short stint on a PCO project, then assign him to what was labelled the Water Interdiction Working Group. Dan Carpenter was our new man for that job. We sent Chief Inspector Burnham, head of the RCMP detachment in Vancouver—a man with experience in anti-drug operations—to the air interdiction group. Cabinet was less interested in Burnham's involvement; he served our purposes nicely, though. He was well known to drug enforcement officials in the U.S. and could attend meetings in Washington without drawing attention to himself."

"Dan, of course, represented the perfect combination of industry savvy and *chutzpah* for the job," Charles said.

"Yes, he's been first rate. I'm sure you can see now why I can't release Dan completely just yet, although I think his work on the task force will come to an end soon."

"Why do you say that?"

"The war on drugs theme has lost a lot of its lustre over the last few months," Lavigne replied. "The president feels he's made his point about sharing hemispheric responsibility. Even though everyone has agreed to wind down the task force before the U.S. election campaign begins, the PM does not want us to be the first to pull the plug. It's time, in any case, to come up with another approach to the drug trade. The cartels are switching tactics again, and the sea route through the closer islands is much less important now to the drug traffic than movements out of Buenos Aires and Montevideo."

Lavigne stopped speaking as the waiter approached with coffee. It was a chance for Charles to regroup his thoughts and he took full advantage of the imposed silence. Lavigne picked at the edges of his partially eaten salad.

Although the Auditor General's Office might not like what it was going to hear from the strict perspective of the Financial Administration Act, the confusion over the Washington/Barbados expenses could now easily be explained in terms of "needs must." The PCO, Charles assumed, must have decided that a small measure of deception on Dan's travel expenses was worth the minor risk of detection by other central agencies. Especially when you take into account the aim of maintaining secrecy around an exercise of this importance to the prime minister. Even Dan's apparently "themeless" office now made sense: the secrecy of his true role precluded even a vague hint of the substance of his work. Dan was hardly the type to waste effort creating an elaborate, dummy project. Protected as he was by his superior, Lavigne, and the Clerk of the Privy Council himself, Dan was obviously free to arrange his work life much as he liked—providing, of course, he continued to deliver the goods.

Charles decided to say nothing to Lavigne about his knowledge of the Barbados meeting. Or of the call he had received from the AG's Office. Leaving well enough alone, he'd move on another tack altogether, now that they were free to talk again.

"So, Dan was enthusiastic about having me take on the research and development support issue?"

"Yes, as I said, he felt you'd be excellent for the R&D job."

"How do you think he'll take to working under me again, though, especially after the high profile assignment he's been on?"

"I thought about that myself, so after the Montebello meeting I talked to Dan in the bar about precisely the point you are raising."

"And how'd he react?"

"Dan was strangely subdued throughout the whole discussion. He spoke of being burned out. About welcoming an opportunity to work again with respected colleagues and not having constantly to maintain secrecy in a lonely, solo job. He was genuinely keen to have you in control and to contribute where he could."

"That's a relief to hear."

"You know, I'll be frank with you, while I clearly recognize Dan's talents, I often find his bravado a bit much to take."

"I know what you mean, but he has so much ability."

"I guess I'm old school," Lavigne said. "Steady, loyal performers are more to my taste. I've worked with some of the brightest and best in Ottawa, and I greatly prefer those who are less disposed to show off how talented they are."

Lavigne fell silent for a moment and then took up his reflection on Dan once more. "I must say, however, that the other night I began to feel genuine sympathy for the young man. He's not one to show much sentimentality, as you know, but over a few drinks he surprised me. He said that, for the last several days, he had been quite upset. It seems that a fellow member of the task force, an Argentinean, was killed—shot in the head in Miami. The news, Dan said, had hit him hard."

An Argentinean. On Dan's committee.

"You seem somewhat distracted," Lavigne said. "Are you all right?"

"Fine."

In truth, Charles took in nothing of the remainder of the lunch conversation with Roger Lavigne. He was too preoccupied with his latest insight: he'd convinced himself the initials *JRP* on Dan's card belonged to Jorge Ramillo-Portes.

CHAPTER 7

1

After considering what he had learned from his lunch with Lavigne, Charles found there was no reason to delay reporting to Brisson. He'd keep it simple and respond only to his concern over Dan's expenses. In that case, there seemed no need for a face-to-face meeting, when a phone call would do.

"The explanation for Dan Carpenter's expense account mystery turned out to be quite straightforward," Charles said. "It was a deliberate piece of deception, done with the full blessing of his superiors. It was carried out, apparently, in the interests of respecting an agreement with the U.S. government to keep a certain hemispheric exercise secret. Dan is working on this—"

"I've seen before those excuses for inappropriate actions," Brisson said. "Was it Carpenter who went to Barbados? Or was it someone else?"

"I don't know any details of the Barbados meeting. What must've happened, though, is that someone in the Privy Council Office covered off Dan's travel arrangements to Washington, while Dan went to Barbados on a secret assignment."

"Did anyone *else* from the Canadian government go with 'im?"

"Not that I know of. I doubt it."

His informant's breezy speculation irritated Brisson. "Did you actually *find* something . . . *concrète* . . . that links Carpenter to the Barbados travel? We 'ave known for some time that Carpenter's name is on a room assignment list. But did he, in fact, *attend* a meeting there? What evidence do you have to support your . . . theory . . . about trips to Washington *and* Barbados?"

Charles sensed that the reporting exercise was getting away on him. He felt he had to offer more convincing authority for his information. "Though I don't know how much detail Roger Lavigne will be prepared to divulge, if you need to satisfy yourself that this expense account thing has a simple explanation, I suggest you talk to Dan's boss directly. Once you hear Lavigne confirm that Dan's been working on something the Canadian government—indeed several other countries—have promised to keep secret, I'm sure that will be the end of the matter."

"Good idea," Brisson replied. "I do not doubt what you said, but perhaps it would be best, you know, if I talk with Monsieur Lavigne myself. Perhaps he can answer, at the same time, a couple of other questions that trouble me."

For Chrissake, these bastards never give up.

Brisson made one final try. "From what you understand of Carpenter's role, is it possible that within the last two months, he could also 'ave visit South or Central America on this secret business that you mention?"

Although Charles did not have an answer, he judged that the AG's office would press him harder if he was too equivocal. "I really don't know for sure, of course; it's entirely possible," Charles replied, comfortable with the mealy-mouthed response he had created.

"The AG thanks you for your assistance, Mr. 'Aversham."

2

Charles waited until he was sure the evening exodus from the office was over before getting back to a question left over from his meeting with Mark Gilmore. His former newspaper buddy had confirmed his own belief that two numbers found among the business cards were telephone numbers. They had agreed it made sense to work first on the area code. Charles thought about using the Internet to look up the numbers, but he still favoured the old-fashioned approach to research. Hands on. He took out the phone book and turned to listings of area codes for Canada, the United States and the Caribbean.

Though plenty of area codes started with five he found none that exactly matched the 574 numbers he was looking for. What perverse mind would give 514 to Montreal and 515 to Des Moines, Iowa? Where in hell, then, would 574 be? Nowhere he could see. Charles made a second run through the tightly printed columns.

Charles then tried the country and city list under "Overseas Calls." This layout seemed easier to scan, so he examined each code that contained a five anywhere in the area code. He took a felt marker in his hand.

Algeria—213

Argentina—**54** (but no 7 in the city code for Buenos Aires or Córdoba)

Australia—61

Austria—43

Bangladesh—880

Belgium—32

Bosnia-Herzegovina—367

Brazil—**5** (*Again no seven in the city codes.*)

Chile—**56**

Seeing a pattern for South America, Charles shot ahead.

Colombia—**57**.

Bogotá, he noticed, added a one; Medellin a four.

The hairs on his neck bristled: **574**. *That's the bloody Medellin country and city code Dan has there in his cards. What in God's name is he up to?*

3

"May I speak with Tom Adams?"

André Brisson had placed a call to a contact in the Canadian Security Intelligence Service, minutes after his conversation with Roger Lavigne.

"Hello, Tom. André Brisson, Principal, Audit Group—from the Office of the Auditor General."

"Yes, I remember you," Adams replied. Long-time senior division chief in the Security Service, he looked like a typical sixties astronaut: same brush cut, same intense eyes. Unlike many astronauts, however, Adams was ex-navy. Ex-RCMP, too. Now he headed a group code-named "Trust Unit," a collection of officers specializing in international white-collar crime. He smiled at the earnestness of his caller's introduction.

"You ask' me several weeks ago," Brisson said, "very unofficially of course, if our review of departmental reporting of travel expenses could explain what Dan Carpenter at the Privy Council Office might be doing in Central and South America. At the time, I knew not'ing solid and said so. Now I am not sure. I feel I should alert you on what has arrive' with that file."

"Sure, go ahead."

"We have been trying to clarify a mystery with Carpenter's travel expenses," Brisson began. "At first, I t'ought we made progress, now the matter is not clear. Perhaps we chose the wrong person."

"You mean someone on your staff?" Adams asked.

"No, someone within PCO. Me, I ask somebody from the inside to look after surveillance for us, but he did not seem to do it right. His report raises more question' than it answers. What can you expect? Not everyone has the precision we develop in our jobs."

"Can you begin at the beginning?" Adams asked, still not sure why Brisson had bothered to call him at this late hour. "I'm having trouble following your drift."

Brisson started over. "Our office 'as been trying to understand 'ow Carpenter could submit travel expenses for a trip to Washington when other evidence from an audit shows dat Carpenter was participating at the same time at an event in Barbados. We 'ave a file that places Carpenter in a meeting in Barbados. We 'ave expenses from the PCO showing Carpenter was at a meeting on the same dates in Washington."

"Got it."

"Yesterday, my PCO contact called to say that Carpenter was on a secret assignment . . . part of a continental task force. The mistake on the expense account could be explain', he said, as a deliberate effort by PCO to . . . to obscure Carpenter's role and activities. He said that travel expenses were for two flights, one to Washington, another to Barbados. He said that, maybe, Carpenter took the trip to Barbados and someone else went to Washington. But PCO sent in only the expenses for the Washington trip."

"So?" Adams interjected.

"When I question' the details, he suggest' I talk to Carpenter's boss. I call' Roger Lavigne today and ask' him directly about Carpenter."

"And did your insider's info prove to be so much bullshit?" Adams asked, now becoming intrigued.

"More or less. Lavigne did confirm—without revealing details— dat Carpenter was working on a 'igh level PCO job. He did not mention, you know, misreporting travel expenses as part of policy. Most important, he said dat Carpenter was never sent to Barbados. *'Une notion absolument folle'* were his exact words. A completely crazy idea."

"Who is the guy with the switcheroo theory, anyway?"

"Charles . . . 'Aversham . . . who was the superior of Carpenter when they were both in the industry department a few years ago. They were in the Defence Production Directorate for a while."

"Interesting," Adams said, as he jotted a note on his pad. "Strange, isn't it, that Haversham gave you the straight goods on some things, then got so far off base with the information on the Barbados trip. Is it possible he knows more than Carpenter's boss does? Or is he trying to get away with a simple story he hopes will respond to your request and sidetrack your investigation?"

Adams did not expect a response. As he commended Brisson for calling, he jotted down another note. He could easily establish the truth of the existence of a task force. Rudimentary enquiries would handle that. Also, it would not hurt to keep an eye on Haversham as well as Carpenter. His team seemed stalled in their efforts in Carpenter's direction. Maybe following up on a connection with Haversham—a connection that now took on more significance, considering which directorate the two men had worked in at Industry Canada—would assist in their investigation.

Adams decided to pass this one on to Lucie Desjardins, the newly recruited security service officer he had recently selected to help on the Carpenter file.

CHAPTER 8

1

Charles looked up from his desk, startled at the sight of the person about whom he had recently been so deep in thought. Casually yet smartly dressed as always, Dan entered the office and plunked himself down in a chair across from Charles's desk. Some of his old verve and energy seemed to be missing; dark circles framed his eyes. It was as if, having burst into the office full of excitement, Dan was now not quite sure why he was there.

"You feeling okay, Dan?" *The PCO job might be keeping him out of the office; whatever he was doing hardly appeared to be fun.*

Dan seemed about to reply, and then he bent down and retied a shoelace. "If you have a few minutes, Charles," he said at last, "this might be a time to discuss the research and development support issue you've been assigned."

"Oh, sure," Charles said, still adjusting to a professional perspective on his former assistant—away from the target of investigation Dan had represented since last weekend. "Lot of pressure on me now to get up to speed."

"I wanted you to get the R&D file. Had to argue a bit with Lavigne—and then, of course, Coté and Harris—before the decision was taken."

"Lavigne said you were persuasive. What did he have against me?"

"Nothing really. I honestly think he was simply playing the devil's advocate—working himself into feeling comfortable about the choice, perhaps turning it over a little in his mind, just because it wasn't his idea in the first place."

"Strange man."

"Don't worry about it," Dan said. "The good news is the assignment is yours and, if it goes on long enough, we may actually get to work together on it. Wouldn't that be great?" Dan appeared much less tense now, more at ease "in his skin"—as his friends at the Université de Montréal would say. "Just like old times!"

Charles was not prepared for Dan's enthusiasm over the possibility of a joint project. More than that, he was uncomfortable with the contrast between Dan's bold support for him with Lavigne and the deepening conviction he felt that Dan was involved in something—for the moment he would merely call "off-centre." Charles let none of this show. He knew that if he were to learn more, he would have to avoid creating the slightest suspicion in Dan's mind. He echoed Dan's lightness of tone.

"It's terrific that the Dynamic Duo from Industry will be back in the saddle again. Should be fun. I'm certainly looking forward to it. Good God, Dan, it's been a while. We could hook up with some of your exotic playmates one evening after work. I've missed that since you went your way and I went mine."

Charles thought he caught a frown.

"It's a deal," Dan said, in a way that Charles found unexpectedly restrained.

Dan seemed lost in space. "I've been busy since I came over here," he continued. Then, picking up the beat to something closer to his normal fast pace, Dan added: "And, as a matter of fact, I'm busy this afternoon. So let's get down to it, if that's okay with you." With that, Dan launched into his view of problems Charles would face in the coming weeks.

"The trickiest aspect," he contended, "is going to be how to position the special treatment the government intends to continue giving to research and development in emerging high-tech industries."

"Without opening up demand for similar treatment from the mature industry sector," Charles added.

"Exactly. The government wants to move in the direction of tax credits rather than direct subsidies." Tax relief, not cash transfers. This would mean an increasing role for the Department of Finance and less for Industry, Dan was convinced. Finance would be worried about opening the barn door; industry associations would feel more comfortable with their old allies at Industry.

Academic economists increasingly argue that traditional Canadian industry is falling behind the rest of the world in productivity, and that much of the explanation for this is the lower level of innovation—especially innovative processes developed within the firm itself. The challenge, Dan said, would be to find, through what could prove to be a seemingly endless round of private consultation with industry associations and leading firms, a basis for some future assistance to these industries that would be acceptable. Any help the government might want to give would have to be limited and presented as occurring in response to pressures from the World Trade Organization.

"I personally think the WTO negotiations will reach a peak next year. Canada will have to be seen to respond early. And the older industry types," Dan asserted with typical force, "will simply have to sit still and suffer in silence until Canada can get through the current round."

Dan spent a further ten minutes suggesting contacts within the departments of industry and finance and in industry associations he considered useful. He singled out one of the authors of the discussion paper prepared for Lavigne's meeting at Montebello. He identified people who would need to be seen out of courtesy and those he thought would be genuinely helpful.

Charles was impressed with Dan's command of issues and the succinctness with which he summarized his advice. As it became clear that Dan was winding up, Charles's mind turned away from R&D support back to Dan's extracurricular activities. He recalled the uncharacteristic sobriety Dan had shown when he first entered his office, then his boyish delight in the notion they'd be teamed up again. He put this together with Lavigne's account of the solemn post-session drink with Dan at Montebello. *This guy's up and down like a yo-yo.* Charles had to set the ground for more exploration of Dan's office and the chance that might offer to learn more about his colleague's curious behaviour.

"Don't suppose you have any documentation I could use?" Charles asked. "I have the Industry Canada paper prepared for the Montebello getaway, not much else."

"Feel free to look around my office any time you want. I'll look at home for some background papers I wrote a few years ago. Meanwhile look at any material in my credenza. I'm sure you will find something of interest there, if you try hard enough."

2

"We've got a leaker in our midst," Roger Lavigne said as Fred Harris entered his office.

"I don't doubt your word, sir, but what makes you think that?"

"The Auditor General's Office is sniffing around again. Now they're interested in Dan Carpenter."

"What is it this time?"

"I have no idea how much they have. Yesterday André Brisson, a principal in their audit group, asked me about Dan's assignment here and whether he had travelled on PCO business to Barbados."

"Um. I see what you mean," Harris said. "Those guys usually prefer fishing expeditions. Such a direct inquiry. Something or someone had to put the AG onto asking that. But who?"

"Within our office, only the Clerk, you and I, and, of course, Carpenter, know about that trip," Lavigne said, fumbling with an unlit cigarette between his fingers. "Damned sure Brisson didn't get it from any of us."

"Are you sure about Carpenter, sir? Not that he'd do anything deliberately. On the other hand, carelessness, perhaps, in his—"

"Check him out. And while you are at it, watch out for anyone here who appears to have an unusual interest in Dan's work, anyone asking questions about Dan and Barbados in the same breath."

Lavigne appeared to be running though a checklist in his mind. "Alert the Industry Minister's office and . . . I guess that will do, for the moment."

"I'll get right on it, sir," Harris said as he shifted towards the door.

"And, Fred, I need hardly remind you. We cannot afford a mistake. Not now. Not after this length of time!"

"You can count on me."

CHAPTER 9

1

Charles sat at the desk in his den sucking on a lollipop Linda had given him weeks earlier. He cast his mind back to his years as a journalist and wondered if any editor then would have encouraged him to think that the Barbados Caper had the makings of a publishable story. On a few sheets of paper he scribbled answers against the classic questions—who? what? where? when? why?— every journalist is required to pose.

The "who?" part seemed to be the best established. Charles clung to a belief that Dan was involved in some way with Ramillo-Portes. Nevertheless, a case could still be made, especially considering the generous and valuable assistance Dan had given him earlier in the day, that there must be some mistake—that a competent, upwardly mobile guy like Dan could not possibly be involved in anything as circumspect as Charles was now envisaging.

On the other hand, it was also a fact—well almost, since Lavigne had not confirmed it in so many words—that Ramillo-Portes was now dead, likely victim of an assassin in Miami. Dan's connection with Portes was underscored, Charles thought, by his initials in what he took to be a password—secreted in Dan's office—and by the realization that Portes was an invitee to a meeting in Barbados, which Dan also attended. Guilt by association, Charles concluded.

The more Charles laboured to give concreteness to the "what, where, when?" of the story, the more he felt that some of his conclusions—even the one he had so confidently conveyed to Brisson about Dan's participation in a meeting in Barbados—rested more on circumstances and inference than on cold facts that he had verified beyond doubt.

Charles reconstructed what he knew with certainty, taking care to be explicit on the basis for his judgments as he made his notes.

From what he learned from Lavigne, it was clear that Dan's job provided an opportunity for Dan to attend a meeting in Barbados but submit expenses for a trip to Washington; the secrecy game the PMO/PCO was playing to please the Americans made that quite plausible. "Not fully verified," he noted against the observation. The AG's file showed Dan had been invited to a meeting; Ramillo-Portes had been invited to the same meeting. He had not confirmed, he now admitted, that Dan *met* with Portes in Barbados.

Although the specifics of the "what and where" were missing, there was hardly any doubt that Dan (most likely along with Portes) was in some way involved with Colombian drug dealers: the Medellin phone number, the nature of the work in which both Carpenter and Portes were involved, and—yes—the hidden numbers in Dan's office that could be a password or PIN made up of Dan and Portes's initials as well as a bank card number. All of these clues appeared to add up to a partnership in some kind of drug-related crime. Charles underscored *appears* in his notes. He could not bring himself to close the loop—not yet.

The "why" part of the story was thus far a complete washout.

- Why was Portes killed? Not a clue.

- Could a drug cartel have killed him? Or others? For money he got from a cartel? Who's to say, at this point?

- Why would Dan get involved in anything remotely like this scenario? Ditto.

- Was anyone else in PCO or from the Canadian side in general involved in the caper? Ditto again.

Charles was disappointed when he realized where rigorous examination had taken his assessment of the status of the Carpenter case. It was tempting to conclude that in reality he had little more than suspicions. It was tempting to forget his preoccupation with Dan and his activities and return to normal.

It was tempting, not characteristic. Charles had long ago experienced the frustrations of investigative journalism—the brief excitement of early revelations, the protracted drudgery of substantiation. He had been too much the consummate professional to give up so easily, simply because all of the pieces of some puzzle refused to fall into place. His mind turned to things left to explore.

Again, he made a list—this time of items he should follow up on next:

- Unidentified computer access number among Dan's cards (What computer could it be??)

- Medellin area telephone numbers—CHECK

- Anything overlooked in Dan's office? (Look again!)

- Dan's secretary (loose lips??)

Charles put down his pen and reviewed his two sets of notes. His re-assessment made the concrete evidence appear even more flimsy on second reading. His "to-do" list seemed pathetically short.

Charles focused on the leftovers. He could talk with Mark Gilmore about the computer access code. He could make a start on Dan's secretary any day now as a legitimate part of his work on the R&D file he had recently been assigned. That would take care of another look around Dan's office as well.

Those Medellin phone numbers remained.

Charles had no idea whether either was Portes's phone number. As matters stood, he knew nothing at all. If he called, he could at least learn something. If one was Portes's phone number, he might get confirmation from either of two possibilities: a voice message or some live answer—from a maid or a family member, for example. If there were no answer—which was also a good possibility, given the news out of Miami—he would be no worse off than he was now.

He dialled the first long distance number and waited. He let the phone ring a dozen or so times. No response. And no answering machine. He hung up, disappointed.

Charles tried the second number. No ring this time. Only a buzz like a connection to a fax machine. He hung up again, dejected that his worst-case scenario had been confirmed.

2

"*Finalmente.* We've had a hit!" An excited young Colombian was speaking to his superior in the Medellin cartel. "I've been sitting here in Portes's apartment for a week, waiting for something, and at last the long-distance call you've been hoping for has come through."

"When'd it arrive? Who was it from?"

"It was only a few minutes ago. I had just begun my watch and was getting a beer from the fridge when I heard the beeps—one long and two short, for a long distance call. So I rushed right over to get the number off that monitoring equipment you had installed. The call was from a guy named Charles Haversham—in the Ottawa area code. In Canada."

Ernesto Cabrillo, the burly cartel group captain, was pleased with the news. Keeping a constant check on Portes's phone calls had been his idea. His bosses had said that Portes's Canadian connection would never call on that phone once he heard that the Argentinean had been taken out. However, Ernesto had argued that because it was Portes's last known address, there was a fair chance his unknown collaborator would become unsettled by the silence and try to contact him there. Besides, he was convinced it would take some time before Portes's partner learned what had actually happened and, since there was no risk to the cartel, it was worth the minimum effort involved to put a man on to monitoring Portes's phone.

Cabrillo put the phone down and addressed the others with a self-satisfied grin: "That prick Portes has finally come through for us. His phone has given up his Canadian accomplice." He strode to the mini-bar, took out a bottle of ice-cold beer, and drained it in one long gulp. "It's only a matter of time now," he said, smiling, "and both those guys will be wasted."

CHAPTER 10

1

Special Adviser (Operations) Charles Haversham had been around the Ottawa scene long enough to expect anything in the arena of lobby group politics. In this case, he was frankly amazed at the rapidity with which events had moved.

It was only a week to the day since Roger Lavigne had asked him to take on the R&D support issue. He had spent almost two days since then completing a few odd tasks he had picked up along the way. He had not yet been able to look through Dan's R&D files. Now he was already invited to a symposium—organized by the International Institute for Studies in World Trade—at the University of Toronto, for no other reason than that somebody with access to the institute's directors knew about his new PCO role.

Topics and speakers were not yet finalized, yet Charles could easily imagine the outcome: the regular stable of academics and professional industry consultants, neatly paired off in familiar set pieces of pro and con presentations—mostly window dressing for the informal lobbying activity that dominates outside the meeting hall. No one would expect him to show the government's whole hand at this early stage. Nevertheless, the professionals working him over would make their preliminary determination of the man and assess the types of arguments to which he appeared most susceptible.

He had to attend. His position required it. Besides, spending a few days at the Toronto conference was not the worst thing he'd have to endure, and so long as you knew what to expect—so long as you didn't mistake attention for a genuine interest in your views— the whole experience could turn out to be quite enjoyable. In fact, as he thought further about the implications of the invitation, Charles began to transform what might have otherwise been only a boring duty into an occasion to serve his own purposes.

The centrepiece of the plan developing in his mind was Dan. Charles would appeal to Lavigne to obtain at least a few days of his former assistant's participation in the conference. They would then be able to work their "Mutt and Jeff routine," as they had called it when they developed it at Industry. "Passive-aggressive spin-doctoring" is more the way they'd put it now.

He and Dan had plenty of time to work out the details of their roles. The key notion was that between the two of them, over the course of the conference, they would learn as much as they could of the positions taken by various industry interests represented there. They would also deliberately contradict each other on possible lines of government's policy responses, sowing confusion among the interests involved. Representatives of the line departments participating in the symposium could be counted on to embellish the kaleidoscope of policy options still further.

Besides having real value for the work, Dan's presence meant, inevitably, debriefing sessions with him at the end of each day. These presented the chance of getting back to a more intimate level of communication—an opportunity, Charles hoped, to penetrate the mystery that increasingly gripped him.

Events had conspired to exacerbate his normal obsessive tendencies. Charles recognized the signs. Wasn't it bad enough that he was now preoccupied with Dan's strange activities even when he was at home? Instead of relaxing in front of the television or reading a good book, what had he done last night? Spent hours working over his "who, what, why list," and then wasted more time with those inconclusive long-distance calls.

Now at work, he could not separate business from his personal fixation. That morning he had arranged with Dan's secretary to have access to his office. Part of his motivation was the obvious need to get on with his work on the R&D file. Dan had offered whatever might be of interest from his bookshelves. His real hope was to find something to fill the huge gaps that still existed in his understanding of the Barbados Caper.

It felt satisfying to have an immediate objective and a clear plan for the Toronto conference that promised to advance his investigation of Dan. Encouraged, Charles called Roger Lavigne and, after some initial resistance from the deputy secretary, successfully negotiated Dan's involvement in the upcoming Toronto conference.

2

"Mr. Carpenter hasn't been in much lately," Dan's secretary, Janet Blair, explained as she swept ahead of him into his empty office. "He has always kept everything so neat and tidy. I'm certain you won't have any trouble finding the papers you need for your project."

"I'll give it a good try."

"Mr. Harris was in here yesterday, and he said he was able to find everything he needed. He wanted access to the filing cabinet, so I opened it for you, too."

"I didn't realize that Fred Harris had anything to do with Dan's work."

"I wouldn't say that they were working together exactly, although he always shows a good deal of interest in what Mr. Carpenter is doing." Nothing in the tone suggested disapproval. On the contrary, a hint of pleasure that dapper Fred Harris was seen around Dan's office as often as he was.

Ms. Blair turned on the desk lamp, opened the blinds, checked the fern on the credenza for dryness, and wheeled to the door. "If there is anything I can help you with, don't hesitate to ask," she said and was gone.

Charles was clear in his own mind that his visit to Dan's office had two purposes. He felt he must use the occasion to examine everything relevant to the R&D file. Then, when he was satisfied that he would not have to ask for access to Dan's room a second time, he could focus on the thing that interested him most—the extent of the risk and reward of Dan Carpenter's secret connection with Jorge Ramillo-Portes. In contrast with his first visit to Dan's office—when he had searched wildly for anything and everything— this time he had a clearer purpose.

When Charles got to the contents of Dan's previously padlocked filing cabinet, he was surprised at the similarity to the office desk he had examined on Saturday morning. Dan was, as his secretary had proudly claimed, a neat and well-organized individual and, to judge from the sparseness of the files normally kept under lock, Dan had perfected the paperless office like no public servant Charles had ever seen.

The bottom section of the two-drawer cabinet was completely empty and the contents of the top drawer filled less than half. At one end were several boxes of high-density diskettes and a package of compact disks—probably more computer games, Charles guessed.

Charles examined the labels on the compact disks. A half-dozen CD-ROMs arranged in numbered sequence bore the main title: "Performance Characteristics of the ZB2 Jet Ski." One was subtitled "Manoeuvrability and Buoyancy Simulations," another "Upgrades and Armament Options." These were far more significant than computer games. Their presence in the padlocked cabinet suggested that much. Charles was curious to know their contents. He needed the privacy of his own room for this task.

He withdrew one of the jet ski CD-ROMs from the filing cabinet and removed it from its jewel case. Then he went to Dan's desk, pulled out a game CD, and used its cover for the jet ski CD. Charles was nervous, now—more flustered than he had expected to be under pressure. His hands shook as he placed the game CD back in the drawer. *How comforting a dram of Scotch would be at this moment.* In his haste to complete the swap, he slammed the desk drawer with a resounding thwack. Uneasy, he looked around to confirm that Dan's office door was shut. Satisfied that no one had heard the bang, he paused for an instant at the door and then casually returned to his own office. There he inserted the compact disk in his computer and sat back in his chair to study the monitor screen.

Charles had not anticipated that the language of the CD-ROM would be Spanish. The graphics, interspersed with short segments of high quality, sharp focus video, bore all the marks of expensively produced, computerized presentations he had seen at Industry. The more entranced he became with the sophistication of the graphics and video, the more the Spanish sound track grated. The narration appeared to be out of sync, the sound muffled. Produced by Logiciels Arcand, a Montreal imaging firm, the CD seemed poorly done, almost amateurish. Charles could not understand the Spanish in any case. He would need to see if Dan had an English version.

Intrigued by his new discovery and emboldened by his earlier success, he returned to Dan's office and removed the full set of compact disks from the security cabinet.

The English language CD-ROM, which his computer now displayed, was of consistently high quality. The graphics were the same as he had seen on the Spanish version, extremely well done. In this case, however, the sound matched the picture in perfect synchronization.

Though he now understood the full meaning of the presentation, Charles was barely further ahead. The purpose of the CDs appeared to be a sales presentation—an impressive effort to promote a product that its manufacturers claimed was state-of-the-art. What was Dan doing with a sales presentation for a souped-up Jet Ski? Was it something he had brought with him from his last job at Industry? What, if anything, did it have to do with his job in PCO? Perhaps the existence of a Spanish version meant that there was some connection to his work on the task force. But what?

As he returned the CD-ROM to its container, Charles noted the company preparing the English version of the CDs was different from the one producing the Spanish. The CD he had just played—in fact, all but one other of the total presentation set—had been made in Toronto by Digital Imaging Corporation.

Charles found it curious that someone had decided to divide the contract this way, despite the fact he'd seen many decisions at least as strange since coming to Ottawa. Possibly some interference from the industry department or even, God knows, Foreign Affairs and International Trade. It was of no great moment anyway. His overriding concern, at this point, was to get the CDs back into Dan's filing cabinet before his secretary locked it for the night.

Again, he entered Dan's office.

Charles was careful to ensure that everything went back where it belonged. First, he returned the five CD-ROMs he had taken from the security cabinet on his second trip. Then he switched back the jewel case covers of the game CD and the Spanish version of the presentation. When he was satisfied that the filing cabinet was as he found it, he opened the top drawer of Dan's desk and placed the game CD in its original spot.

Dan's desk drawer jammed as Charles attempted to slide it shut. Kneeling before the desk, he reached in to feel the drawer tracks. Stuck between a slider track and the desk wall lay the explanation— a small package wrapped in soft plastic and sticky tape.

Charles did not need a reporter's experience to tell him that the hidden package was important. While he knew he had to examine it, he also knew not to take unnecessary chances. He'd been more than a little cavalier in his running back and forth between offices that afternoon. Someone was bound to notice his peculiar behaviour. Besides, Janet Blair would want to lock the cabinet and close up before long. Charles felt he had no choice but to remove the package, at least temporarily, from the office.

The risk to himself, he fully appreciated, was greater than anything he had yet encountered. His Saturday morning visit to Dan's office might have proved somewhat awkward, if forced to explain his presence in a colleague's office. Nothing compared to his current situation.

Charles imagined being caught red-handed trying to get the package back into Dan's desk. He put himself into Dan's shoes. No bloody reason, Dan would say, for looking in his desk in the first place. No excuse for taking anything from his desk drawer. Not the faintest legitimate excuse for removing the package from the office altogether. Dan would be left with one obvious inference: the colleague now standing shamefaced in front of him must have some grounds for being suspicious of his behaviour. Under the weight of all this evidence, Dan could not have avoided the conclusion that Charles was investigating him. He would feel betrayed by a friend.

The burden of that prospect weighed on Charles's conscience. It was worth taking a moment to ponder his next move.

At that instant, he had to admit, he did not actually know the full scope of the situation Dan had put himself in—he expected the package to reveal much on that score. He did recognize, however, that the more serious the situation, the more aggressive Dan's protective response would be, once he sensed danger.

Charles thought briefly about Portes's death in Miami and wondered for a moment if Dan was in so deep he could even have been responsible for that. Then he thought about his own position: acting entirely alone, without credentials or commission, driven forward by nothing more than raging curiosity. Charles thought about these things, especially the extreme vulnerability they implied.

Screw it. I've come too far to chicken out now.

Charles pocketed the plastic-wrapped object and casually strolled out of Dan's office, down the corridor, into the tranquility of his own office.

CHAPTER 11

1

Two hours passed before Charles could examine the contents of the concealed package. First, he had a visit from the two authors of the paper on R&D subsidies from Industry Canada. Then he had fielded a call from the senior editor of the *Globe and Mail*'s Report on Business, who had already received word of his upcoming participation in the Toronto World Trade Symposium. Charles dealt with both "intrusions" with as much dispatch as he felt appropriate. Finally, at ten past five, after his secretary stuck her head through the door to announce her departure for the day, Charles got down to examining the contents of Dan's mysterious package: a 2DD IBM floppy disk, 720 kb capacity. No label.

All thumbs in anticipation, Charles introduced the floppy into his A drive and waited for the monitor to display its contents.

Charles could scarcely believe it. The floppy contained a series of e-mail exchanges between Portes and Carpenter, taking place over what appeared to be more than half a year. Charles scanned the file titles and examined each message in turn. The plot line was as evident as it was incriminating.

It was Portes, as it turned out, whom the cartel first contacted. In one of his early e-mails, Portes told Dan that the drug bosses already knew all about the supposedly hush-hush international committee against drug traffic. More. Portes further revealed that the cartel had a general picture of the working group's approach, confirmed at the Barbados meeting. Canadian-built Jet Skis—transported by Canadian-made floatplanes—had emerged as an integral part of the shore patrol plan. The cartel wanted detailed information to assess the seriousness of the threat to its operations. They were particularly interested in the capabilities of the Jet Skis.

Portes, the record showed, handled all the direct contacts with the cartel. Dan had the detailed information on the Jet Skis. Opportunity merged with inclination and, out of the mix, the two friends developed a scheme to line their pockets.

Charles skipped through the next exchanges of e-mails until he came upon an explanation of the Spanish version of the Jet Ski presentation. It was Dan's idea to re-dub a Spanish voice over an English-language presentation—over the CD-ROMs prepared for the task force. Together they added some detail of their own on the planes involved, to put the shore patrol equipment in context.

Portes was less than enthusiastic over the quality of the product Dan had been able to produce in Spanish. Despite this, he appeared to have gone ahead with the delivery, since the next reference in the e-mails was to a deposit of the cartel's payoff to Portes's bank account. Portes assured Dan that he had transferred Dan's half share of the first installment to his partner's account.

Charles was well into his viewing of files on the diskette when the phone rang.

"Oh, Mr. Haversham," said the voice at the other end, "you're still there. Good. If it's convenient now, Mr. Lavigne would like to have a word with you in his office."

Damned inconvenient. "I'll be there in about ten minutes. Shutting things down for the day."

Charles had no idea what was up. Or how long the "word" with Lavigne would take. He was in no mood to take any chances. He removed the diskette from the A drive and locked it in his desk. For good measure, he logged off his computer.

2

Lavigne was unusually chatty, considering the time of day. Charles wanted nothing more than to return to more engaging subject matter awaiting him in his office. The deputy secretary, on the other hand, was in an expansive mood and wished to share his views on the forthcoming symposium in Toronto.

He'd been thinking about the likely timing of the government's response on R&D subsidies and was now worried, he said, that anything that might be conveyed to the industry associations on the subject would raise unrealistic expectations over the speed with which action might be taken. It was, after all, a new day—and the high priority accorded the file only a week or so ago had now been replaced by an even more urgent concern. It would be best, he advised, to say as little as possible at this time.

"Dan and I are not going to give much away, I assure you. Even if the issue were still number one, it is not my style to be too forthcoming with interest groups. 'More blessed to receive than to give' is my motto in these matters. And what we propose to give them, they'll have trouble adding up to something tangible. That's the approach to our participation in the symposium I propose we follow even more rigorously now, considering what you have just said. I assume that has your approval."

"Yes, that's fine," Lavigne said, "but your mention of Dan reminds me of another point. When I spoke to him about attending the Toronto conference with you, he asked if he could skip opening day and attend only the second. He says he still has a few loose ends to finish up and may, in fact, have to travel quite a bit over the next few weeks. Says he can't spare the time for the full conference."

Disappointment showed immediately on Charles's face. His plan required—absolutely—at least one evening alone with Dan. *I'm going to fight for it.*

"Look, I know Dan has other things to do, and I don't want to overload him. However, if we are to assemble the intelligence I need to do *my* job, I need at least one evening of his time."

Lavigne seemed unmoved.

"You know as well as I do that it's the informal side—drinks and dinner after the formal sessions are over—that makes attendance at these affairs even halfway useful. Best time to listen to what's on their minds. Best chance for us to play our game, too. Can we compromise? May I have Dan for the second conference day and at least through to breakfast the next morning?"

Lavigne paused for a moment and then showed a mere hint of a smile. The first smile Charles had seen from the stolid deputy secretary. "Okay," he said, "I will concede—occasionally—to a convincing argument. The disinformation approach you're proposing *will* work better if both of you are involved. I'll inform Dan tomorrow of my agreement with your request."

"Thank you."

"Keep me informed of your preparations."

3

Although it was well past six when he got back to his office—and he and Diane were down for dinner together at home—Charles could not resist getting back to Dan's e-mails. Without bothering to make notes of his meeting with Lavigne, he booted up his computer, entered his password, introduced Dan's diskette again into his A drive, and searched the files for the spot where he had left off. As he opened the e-mail in which Portes reported delivery of the Jet Ski presentation to the drug bosses, a question burst into Charles's consciousness. How did those guys manage to get the Spanish presentation CDs to their "clients"? No mention in e-mails about Dan or Portes travelling. Surely, they would not have risked the mail or a courier service. How, then, could they have done it? And, it appears, so quickly?

Perhaps it was the recent experience of logging on to his own computer, or maybe it was his fascination with the high technology solution Dan had found to their "presentation requirement." Whatever it was, Charles had a hunch on a detail that had blanked him so far. Charles needed to consult with Mark. He rang his friend at home.

"Mark? Charles. Got a minute? I need to pick your brains on the technical feasibility of something. I'm sure you'll be able to help me out."

Without waiting for a response, Inspector Haversham went on to outline his new theory. He reminded Mark of the five cards with the numbers, their discussion of the probability that two were telephone numbers, and their belief that two cards might be related to bank funds. Then he got to the real purpose of his call.

"What I need to know now, Mark, is the answer to this simple question. Is it possible to access a remote computer and download the contents of a CD-ROM over a phone line? Can a computer at the other end pick up the transmission and produce a CD that is a perfect match of the original? Let's make it even more complicated. Can you download the contents of more than one CD in this way?"

"Sure thing," Mark replied without hesitation. "First the two communicators would need modems attached to their computers. Then they would require the appropriate software on the receiving end—a couple of efficient software packages exist—that basically picks up the CD transmission and allows a duplicate CD to be burned at the receiving end. The second or third CD is not a problem, in principle. Someone would have to be standing by at the receiving end to insert additional blank CDs, on signal, at the right time."

"Fantastic! And what, technically speaking, would be involved in making a connection with a remote computer in the first place?"

"That's perfectly straightforward. First, you need a telephone number for the computer modem. Then most systems require both an access code and a user ID—normally two sets of data input, simply to assure greater security."

"Would a typical access code be as complex as the one on card number one? That jumble of symbols and numbers?"

"Absolutely."

"Damn. I can't thank you enough, Mark. All I have to do now is confirm which card has the user ID and figure out which is the phone number for the modem."

CHAPTER 12

1

"What's buggin' you, Charlie?" Diane demanded, her voice at least a half octave above normal. Dressed all in black, her dark hair pulled back with an ebony barrette, she looked a perfect match between her appearance and her mood. "You've been pushing that damned lamb chop all over your plate. And you haven't touched your wine. Something must be seriously wrong if you're not drinkin' with me."

Typical shot, Charles thought, without responding. Pissed off again, he figured, because he was late getting home; and half-pissed from a few too many cocktails before dinner.

Rather than provoke Diane further, he fashioned a conciliatory response. "Look . . . I'm sorry if I seem a bit . . . distant . . . tonight. I admit that I haven't been the . . . the easiest person to live with lately."

"Well," Diane shouted, "the Great Communicator doth finally pronounce. You know, for someone who used to earn a living with words, you sure are the pits when it comes to saying anything meaningful at a personal level. 'Not the easiest person to live with.' What a pile of clichéd crap!"

Charles held his tongue as her rant continued. "It's bad enough you have no interest in me any more. You hive yourself off in that damned den of yours night after night. Worse, you can't even manage some sensible, adult conversation on the one evening of the week we're alone without Linda."

"Come on, Diane."

"You're a total zero as a husband and you're not much better as a father," Diane said, choking back tears of frustration. "You're interested only in your job. At least you seem to spend a hell of a lot of time working at it. But if you are as inept at it as you are at home, your career'll be even shorter than our miserable marriage."

Her implied threat to end their marriage signalled that the battle was nearly over. Probably one more volley, Charles anticipated. Most likely, a reference to her high hopes when he came home and told her about Professor Bart's "job offer." Or maybe her disappointment that the Ottawa he had made seem so interesting when he had written about it as a journalist was not half as exciting when one actually had to live in the dreary place. Something nostalgic, something revealing of an intense sadness that so often ambushed her whenever she got well into the sauce.

Tonight, however, Diane went no further than the breakup threat; instead, she sat, spinning her wineglass through her fingers, staring at her own partially eaten dinner. Sullen.

"Something's been eating at me for a while," Charles admitted, "and I am genuinely sorry that it has affected you—and I suppose Linda, too. It's not about work, as you might think. Well, it is and it isn't. You see it's about someone at work . . . I need to talk about it, if you'll listen."

Diane glared at Charles. Now she was certain she knew why he was acting so calmly, why he had refused to rise to the bait and strike back with bitter sarcasm. He'd been having an affair with someone at the office. For weeks, if not longer, she was sure. Diane imagined Charles's next move: Now the son of a bitch plans to use *her* blow-up to segue into a "confession" (*surely he wouldn't have the balls to do something drastic here and now*) or maybe to present some "explanation" for his behaviour that would inevitably end up placing the blame on her.

A small caution light went off before Diane's eyes. Amusing as it would be to jerk her husband's chain, she had to be careful that her provocation did not go so far as to expose the vulnerability of her own position. Linda had told her of the call from the Montreal hotel room and her daddy's surprised reaction that she was not there. She had indeed been absent only for a short time while she conferred, over afternoon tea, with her sister, on the choice of restaurants for the evening. On the other hand, Diane knew the Montreal trip would not stand up to detailed scrutiny, if Linda had inadvertently "inspired" Charles sufficiently to enable him to dissect her chance encounter in the hotel bar that evening and her contorted effort to slide into bed without waking Linda later that night.

"Go ahead, I'm listening," she said after a long pause.

For an instant, Charles hesitated, recognizing the insincerity in his wife's tone. Common sense told him that he should save it for another day, when she'd had less to drink—or keep what he was about to say forever to himself. However, Charles was also excited about his discovery and, now that he had an audience, he could not give up easily the chance to share it.

He began with the call from the AG, touched on his visit to Dan's office, and skipped lightly over the set of numbers he found hidden there. He justified his early fear that Dan Carpenter was involved in something far more serious than travel expense fraud mostly from information he had received from Lavigne. Charles found himself repeating the report of Portes's assassination in Miami and the strong effect that news of it had evidently had on Dan. Subconsciously, Charles kept returning to a key element in his conversion to suspicion.

As Charles's unfolding of the Carpenter story came closer to finding the computer diskette hidden in Dan's desk, he studded his account with more detail.

"For a long while I'd nothing more than some type of password to link Portes and Dan in something suspicious-looking, but I didn't know what. Then today, when I was consulting some files in his office, I found clear evidence he and Portes had been selling information—if you can believe it—to one of the Colombian drug cartels. Both were members of an international committee working on ways to improve the interception of drug shipments. They decided, at some point, to turn inside knowledge into cash."

"How in heaven's name did you come to that conclusion?" Diane blurted, now fully drawn into Charles's story.

"Dan kept an electronic record of his e-mail exchanges with Portes. I found them on a diskette he kept hidden in his office desk. I must've jarred it loose when I was looking in his desk. In any case, I've been able to piece together a fairly coherent picture of what they've been up to."

"For Chrissake, Charlie. That's not like you, snooping around in somebody else's desk."

"I know. It's not something I'm proud of, but honest to God, once I got started on this, I haven't been able to stop."

"Well, anyway, go on," Diane said, eager to hear more of his discoveries, even if she disapproved of his methods.

"A Medellin cartel member approached Portes saying that he needed detailed information on the equipment to be used in the task force's plan. Dan and Jorge agreed to provide it—for a price. Portes was the contact. Carpenter was the one with detailed knowledge of the Jet Skis. Dan controlled the production of a CD-based presentation originally put together for the Canadian government to sell the idea to the task force. Cleverly, Dan and Jorge made their own Spanish language version of the CDs and sold it to bloody drug bosses."

Diane looked dumbfounded.

"With me so far, Diane?"

"Go on. It's a lot more interesting than the usual stuff you cart home."

Charles ignored her arrow and carried on.

"Late this afternoon I had a hot hunch. I've been unable to get anywhere with one set of numbers on the cards in Dan's office. Then, all of a sudden this afternoon, I got it."

"What?"

"Dan was able to send the contents of the Spanish version of the CD presentation to Portes electronically. No travel. No risk of a customs inspection. Dan simply telephoned Portes's modem. Then, he set up a computer-to-computer download of the CDs. From Ottawa to Colombia in the flash of an eye."

"Sounds far-fetched."

"I'm absolutely sure of it," Charles said. " I tested the connection myself tonight before leaving the office. I didn't send anything. However, I did establish a link with Portes's computer using the numbers Dan had written on those cards. The important thing is, it worked."

"That's why you were so late. Farting around with talking computers at the office."

"I discovered, too, that they didn't download only once. The most recent e-mail exchanges show the Medellin gang wanted more information after they saw the CD-ROM presentation. Portes pressed Dan to send detailed data giving all the technical specs on the special equipment on the Jet Ski. Dan sent everything computer-to-computer again. Amazing. Neat technology, eh?"

"How long ago did all this happen? Are we talking weeks or years, here?"

Charles's excitement over his detailed disclosure of the results of his investigation showed in his flushed face and rapid speech. "The e-mails say about two months ago."

"Wow."

Charles knew he had a captive listener now. "Somewhere along the line the Colombians appear to have become less enthusiastic for their side of the bargain. Interesting thing," Charles said after a pause in which he appeared to go within himself for a spell of reflection, "there's no explanation for it in the e-mails. Not another word from Portes, in fact, until a few weeks ago, maybe the very day he was killed. In the end, it proved to be a severe understatement. Portes wrote: 'Miami unfriendly. Stay home until you hear from me again'—or words to that effect."

"God. Do you suppose Dan is in danger, too?" Diane asked.

"I've been asking myself that as well. I assume he is, though I frankly don't know how I can prove it. And that's not the only thing I wonder about. Why would Dan need to meet with Portes in Miami? And what could've gone wrong with the deal to upset the Colombians enough to assassinate Portes? If I knew the answer to this one, I'd know how much danger he's in."

"Hell," Diane snapped, "I'm bothered by an even more important question. Why would Dan get involved with a thing like this in the first place?"

"Damned if I know," Charles admitted. "I intend to get to the bottom of it when I confront Dan at a conference at the University of Toronto end of next week."

Charles surveyed the cold lamb chop and limp beans on his plate. Unappetizing as they looked earlier, they were now strangely appealing to him. He reached for salt and pepper, and doused his plate liberally. He filled his glass with red wine. Then he demolished the remaining contents of his plate with more obvious enjoyment than he had shown for any meal in a week.

"Good dinner," Charles said.

"First dinner conversation in months," Diane said.

2

From the black Ford sedan parked on Patterson Avenue, two car lengths back from the corner of Metcalfe, Lucie Desjardins had an unobstructed view of the entrance to the Havershams' house. The young, dark-haired CSIS officer had taken up her lookout position at 10 p.m., as she had every night that week. Tonight she shifted uneasily in her seat, hoping that this watch would be more eventful than the previous ones.

Lucie had come to her CSIS job by a roundabout route. One of six children born to her mother, Lucille, she was the last of the first trilogy, so to speak—a mere five-year-old when her father was killed. Albert Desjardins, an Ontario Provincial Police officer in Sudbury, had single-handedly attempted to arrest a drink-crazed trapper in the Long Lake area and received a bullet in the neck for his efforts. Lucie's grief at the loss of her loving father was matched in intensity only by that of her mother. Whereas Lucie committed years to the nurture of her father's memory, Lucille found early consolation in the arms of a widowed neighbour, Mike Symanski, and married again within a year.

Lucie's revulsion over her mother's decision exacerbated her isolation in the Symanski household. A boy, another boy and then a little sister followed in rapid succession, leaving Lucie—like so much stale meat filling in a sandwich—feeling unwanted and ultimately rejected.

After high school, Lucie moved out. Seeking as much distance as she could from her family, she changed her name back to Desjardins (she never forgave her Mom for saddling her with Symanski), and set herself on a course—first as a part-time student at Algonquin College and then as a criminology student at the University of Ottawa—towards a professional career in law enforcement.

To support herself at school, Lucie worked as a waitress at a late night beehive for many young jocks in the city, drawn by the food, the atmosphere, and a serving staff that would easily have met the appearance standards for Hooter's. Lucie soon learned to control the young bucks that mistook her sultry beauty for an invitation to grab, and before long was both the longest standing employee in the bar and the waitress with the highest weekly gross in tips.

After graduation, Lucie stayed in her first "real job" for only a few months. Though delighted at gaining a starting position in the RCMP's White Collar Crime Unit, Lucie soon discovered that the slow pace of what was essentially research rather than investigation bored her beyond words. She had joined the RCMP for action, not sitting at a desk manipulating a computer. She recognized, of course, that she would be taking a risk in moving on so soon from her first appointment. However, when she heard through the office grapevine of the establishment of a new RCMP-CSIS combined operation on international white collar crime, she leapt at the opportunity to express her interest.

Tonight, her second successful job interview since graduation already felt like a mistake. To date, her work in the Trust Unit—known affectionately among members of the group as the "Funny Money Gang"—had been scarcely more adventurous than her previous assignments. Worse, whereas at the RCMP she always felt she could see the rationale for her tasks, now the whole thing seemed poorly defined, if not downright silly.

Her job was simply to observe Charles Haversham: note all comings and goings in the evening at his home, photograph arrivals and departures with an infrared camera, post the time, and report to HQ at the end of her five-hour shift. From nothing more than his file that she had reviewed before beginning her first night's observation, Lucie had formed a largely positive opinion of her subject. Only his propensity to seek the company of prostitutes while away from home on government business stood out in bold relief. Nothing else in his record set off alarm bells in her (admittedly inexperienced) head. Her new charge's involvement in athletics as a youth and his career transition from journalist to executive-level public servant reflected enough of her own achievement and aspiration to reinforce the favourable response she felt on first seeing his flattering photograph.

Lucie felt strongly that Stan Parker, her immediate superior in the working group, had failed to convey any sense of purpose in her new job description. "We're watching Haversham because the boss has asked us to watch Haversham. End of story," Parker had said finally, when he had grown tired of Lucie's insistent appeals for details.

His treatment of what she considered a reasonable request for clarification grated, especially since Parker had been assigned Dan

Carpenter. From the minimal briefing she received, Lucie saw Carpenter as a much bigger fish in the investigation. Tracking him, she was convinced, was more like the level of challenge she wanted for herself. She was annoyed at the clear difference in importance between her job and Parker's, and had not been reluctant to say so. Her probationary status did not seem to affect her willingness to express an opinion one bit.

"You'll get used to following orders, kid," was how Parker summed up their conversation. "We all do eventually." That was the closest her supervisor could come to a hint of sympathy for her frustrated expression.

At 11 p.m., the lights went out in the Haversham household. Another uneventful watch, Lucie thought. Except for a car that had driven in from the Parkway, turned around and parked a block further up the street, there'd been no movement whatever on the quiet residential street since she arrived. No one left the house. No one entered.

Keeping one eye on the Haversham house, the young agent recruit made herself as comfortable as possible under the circumstances and let her mind wander over preparations for her older sister's forthcoming wedding. She was not looking forward to the family reunion, but her sense of loyalty to a sister who suffered silently, yet almost as deeply as herself, was critical in her decision to attend. She worried about her meeting with her mother and she feared an encounter with her stepfather. Bitter memories of confrontation flooded over her. Lucie Desjardins did not notice the midnight departure of the car parked farther up the street.

3

Rocco Pauli, the driver of the car, had now settled a few things and raised a few doubts.

He had confirmed a match between the phone number picked up in the Medellin area and Haversham's home address. That was the easy part. The reverse directory gave the address and an enquiry with neighbours established that the Haversham family—Charles, Diane and their daughter, Linda—currently occupied the house.

Rocco had also realized that he was not the only one interested in Charles Haversham. He had noticed what might be a stakeout car the previous evening, during an observation session of his own. The repeat visit to Patterson Avenue that night confirmed his suspicions. He assumed it was the RCMP.

Rocco shifted his 250-pound frame uncomfortably from cheek to cheek. Then he chewed the end of his half-smoked Tueros. Nobody had mentioned anything to him about police involvement. On the contrary, his cartel contact had made it sound so simple. "We want you to find a prick who screwed up on a deal with us," a Medellin cartel intermediary had said. "Then knock off the son of a bitch so there's no link back to us."

"A broken drug deal?" Rocco had asked.

"Nothing like that," his contact had replied. "You don't need to know. You're in 'cause you got no connections with the cartel. And for the clean job you did on a few of the Rock Machine in Montreal. Should be a piece of cake."

Now, Rocco felt things were more complicated. Did the RCMP have Haversham under surveillance or were they offering him protection from his enemies? *Damn, I'm as ready as the best of them to make the bastard. But I ain't doin' it, if Haversham is a fuckin' double agent or something.*

This thought led him to another conclusion. He would get back to his contact to report on the new situation and await further orders.

CHAPTER 13

The preliminary program for the Toronto conference sat unopened on his desk. Charles was not ignoring the event. Indeed, he'd been working hard that morning on implementing some of Dan's suggestions on R&D support, although he cared little about the formal topics. His chief concern was the best approach to the consultative process surrounding the event, especially now that Dan would be there for less time. He wanted to prove himself to Lavigne.

The files that Dan had made available in his office had provided invaluable background. So useful, in fact, that Charles had asked Dan's secretary for access to his office the next day to check a particularly helpful reference. Charles took advantage of the situation to return the diskette, undetected, to its original hiding place in Dan's still unlocked desk.

It was a relief to be able to concentrate on the job for a change. Charles had concluded there was nothing more he could do with the Barbados Caper until he could get Dan alone in Toronto. In the meantime, he would do what the good taxpayers of Canada were paying him to do—earn his keep as a public servant in a position of some responsibility. For the first time since André Brisson called him from the Auditor General's Office, Charles felt relaxed. He was free of mind-twisting conundrums. Only a feeling of calm and well-being, as he got deeper into his work.

The mood did not last.

André Brisson was on the line. "Look 'Aversham . . . er . . . Charles," he said, starting in a hesitant manner that contrasted strongly with the confidence he had displayed in their earlier conversations. "I been wondering whether to call you or not, but I 'ave decide' I owe it to you. Perhaps I was wrong, you know, to recruit you to snoop on Dan Carpenter. I feel I was certainly wrong, me, to have been so—how you say—impatient when you called to report on what you had found."

Charles was keen to let the whole business drop, especially now that he appreciated how much more complex the Carpenter affair had become. "No need to apologize," Charles said, "I haven't given it another thought."

"*Bon*. But I feel I must tell you—since you 'ad suggest' that I contact Roger Lavigne to confirm your story—that he deny Carpenter was involved in any meeting in Barbados."

"Oh."

"He 'as verify your information about the nature of his assignment, but he said I was misinformed on Barbados. I t'ought you should know, for what dat is worth."

Charles decided it was best to cut and run. "Sorry," he said, "that I may have caused you any embarrassment with Lavigne. I must admit now that my statement to you was, I suppose, a bit of a deduction from something Lavigne told me. No proof, in fact. That'll teach me to be more careful another time," Charles added, mostly to fill the long silence at the other end of the line.

The feebleness of Charles's admission disturbed Brisson's controlled demeanour. Now the audit principal was in no mood to apologize. In fact, he regretted his decision to call. Bringing the conversation to a sudden halt, he said, "I guess we are both agreed, it was a mistake to involve you in our investigation of PCO expense reporting. You can count on it, it will not happen again."

As he put down the receiver, Charles was unfazed by Brisson's uncharacteristic rudeness. He was still smarting over the manner in which an official in the AG's Office had so confidently assumed that if the office wants you to do something, you'll comply. What bothered Charles most was the way he had caved in so readily to that expectation.

Strangely, Charles did not see a problem with his own investigation of a colleague that had already become more invasive than anything Brisson had asked him to do. That, he had rationalized to his satisfaction, was a different matter altogether. His was an investigation based on pure reason—an indulgence in the search for truth for truth's sake. No harm could come, Charles believed, from a purely intellectual exercise in which the ultimate outcome was the unfolding of the revelation itself.

Once again, the Carpenter affair pushed its way to the centre of Charles's attention. Contrary to what he had told Brisson about its being a guess about Dan's attendance at the Barbados meeting,

Charles knew that the e-mail exchanges had established beyond doubt that this had been the venue for a critical session between the two conspirators. No question in his mind that Dan had gone to Barbados. Why would Lavigne not acknowledge that fact?

Now Charles had a new agenda item, one that took him in a fresh direction: why had Roger Lavigne lied to Brisson?

CHAPTER 14

1

The lead-up to the Toronto symposium was proving a major bore. Charles was not used to constantly fine-tuning his briefing notes. Fred Harris and some others in the office were even revising drafts of the "remarks" he had prepared for possible interventions from the floor. Although he could appreciate the great care taken with everything meant for public consumption, Charles considered the process excessive. It did nothing for his edginess.

Time also weighed heavily on his mind. One day drifted into another with little variation, except for his continuing preoccupation with Dan's mystery. Charles could think only of the chance the Toronto meeting offered to conclude his probe. The event could not come soon enough.

That Dan was never in the office—away somewhere tying up loose ends, as Lavigne had put it—was disconcerting. Almost as puzzling as Lavigne not telling Brisson about the Barbados meeting when he was asked directly. Inevitably, Charles began to stew over these and other unexplained actions that had thus far failed to yield to the discovery of information or the application of imagination.

One thing he came back to, repeatedly, was whether someone else in the federal government was in on Dan's scheme. Earlier, Charles had been quite certain this was not likely; now he was not so sure. A few things made him uneasy.

The new information he had from Brisson now meant that Lavigne was a possibility. Besides creating some suspicion over his concealment from Brisson of Dan's trip to Barbados, Lavigne's lax treatment of Dan had become noteworthy. Lavigne had said the project was about to wind down. So, what was Dan doing roaming around, rarely reporting in? Was Lavigne protecting him in some way?

The idea that Lavigne himself was the kingpin in the Canadian side of the misadventure was as implausible to Charles now as Dan's involvement had seemed earlier. Then Charles had dismissed even the idea of Dan being involved in travel expense fraud, proving, he now supposed, that appearances can be deceiving. In this case he was more certain in his skepticism: Lavigne was, in his own words, too "old school" to be put into the same category as the hedonistic twins, Dan and Jorge.

How then, if not with someone's help, had Dan been able to get the information requested by the cartel so quickly when they asked Portes to provide detailed specs on the ZB2 Jet Ski? If Dan and Portes had the information, would they not have given it to the cartel originally? And if they had to request it later, wouldn't the firm have been suspicious—or at the very least reluctant to respond without checking out the authority level of the person making such a request? Is it possible that someone else—higher up—submitted an urgent demand for information? Was that Lavigne? Or did Dan get some help from his old friends at Industry Canada?

As far as Charles was concerned, Lavigne's fortress was impregnable. He could do something to explore the departmental connection, however, and at least eliminate that as a possibility if it proved so. He immediately remembered Frank Hampton, an old line official who had been around since Industry, Trade and Commerce days. If anyone had an inside track to major Canadian manufacturers, it was Frank. He would know everyone else in the department who could possibly be Dan's source on the ZB2. Charles figured that there was no better place to start than with a phone call.

"Frank, it's Charles Haversham. Remember me?"

"Yeah, sure. How's it goin' over there with the policy types? How long since you've been gone from here . . . half a year?"

"Not that long, Frank. It's been long enough though that I'm a bit rusty on a few things I should know. I hope you can give me some help on that score. I'm working on R&D subsidies in the manufacturing industry and I think you could complete my education."

"I doubt that, sir, but I'm willing to try. What do you want to know?"

Charles had already decided he was going to get to his kicker by a circuitous route. "I'm trying to get a grip on industrial innovation. I know Industry doesn't have much to do with a firm when it's still back in the research mode, but don't you sometimes get involved when things start to move out of research and into product development?"

"True enough. Things haven't changed much over here, Mr. Haversham."

"Okay. So at that stage, say they're looking for some kind of support from the department, how much information would they typically share with you on the product they plan to bring into production?"

"That depends."

"Depends on what, Frank?"

"On what kind of working relationship they've built up over the past—how much they feel they can trust you."

"So, say somebody wanted to see detailed specs for a product that the department had already supported in some way—one that was in the beta production stage. Would you or one of the other guys get to see it, if you asked nicely?"

"Probably. What are you getting at?"

Charles smiled. He was a step away from springing the big one. "Now suppose the product we're talking about here is some new laser technology. Who would be the most likely person in Industry to handle that one?"

"That would be Pierre Leroux," Frank said without hesitation.

"Yes, and if the product was the new ZB2 Jet Ski, who would that be, Frank?"

Dead air.

"Frank, are you there?"

Hampton spoke in a whisper: "Look, they've got me in one of those damn cubicles and it's not convenient to talk."

"Well, can I meet you somewhere? For a beer after work?"

"I suppose," Frank said. After a pause: "But not tonight. I've got bowling at seven and I have to get home for supper."

"Tomorrow, then. How about a beer and smoked meat at Dunn's deli—just across the street for you. Five o'clock?"

"Okay. Don't bring anybody with you. Understand?"

"Sure Frank, I understand . . . geez," Charles added, trying desperately to draw something more from Hampton, "I must have hit a raw nerve. Are you okay?"

Frank was not biting. In fact, he had hung up before Charles had finished his sentence.

2

When Frank Hampton failed to show for the rendezvous at Dunn's, Charles was beside himself. He fretted through two drafts and the Miss Montreal sandwich, waiting until 6:15, when he was sure Frank was not going to appear. A few months earlier, he might have tossed back four or five beers under similar circumstances. Now he was doing better in that department. Ever since he began to look into the Barbados Caper, he found he was not drinking so much. Not even in self-defence on weekends.

His first inclination was to think that his only option was to wait until morning to call Frank at the office. Then he thought of calling him at home. No goddamned excuse about someone overhearing him there, Charles decided, as he entered 240 Sparks Street in search of a payphone. How many Frank Hamptons could there be?

Faced with two options, Charles called the first listed. Francis Hampton responded. Charles got off with a single sentence.

His second call found the right address, just no Frank Hampton. "I'm sorry, Frank is not here," a sweet voice announced at the end of the line. "I'm not expecting him home until about 9:30. This is his bowling night, you see."

"Well, tell him that Charles Haversham called and that I would appreciate a call from him at my office tomorrow morning."

"I'll give him the message. He's been a bit forgetful in the last day or two. I'll be sure to remind him when he leaves for work in the morning."

Forgetful maybe. More like evasive, Charles thought. Now he had another liar on his list.

3

The CBC national news was ending when Charles was jolted awake by the phone ringing near his left ear. He jumped from the couch and grabbed the receiver on the second ring, anxious not to awaken his daughter.

"I don't want you to call me again, Mr. Haversham, or try to get in touch with me," Frank Hampton whispered.

"Frank?" Charles queried, still groggy with sleep.

"I'm not supposed to say a word. I've decided to tell you this much 'cause we've known each other for a long time. I am the departmental contact on the ZB2. You've got to promise me you won't tell anyone I told you. I've had orders. That's why I couldn't talk when you phoned me at the office."

"What's so special about a bloody Jet Ski that you've got the department battening down the hatches at the mere mention of it?"

"I'm not saying anything more. In fact, we're supposed to inform the associate deputy's office if we get so much as a vague inquiry on the subject. I'm not going to do that, either—for old time's sake—but if you keep bugging me, I sure as hell will."

"Don't worry, Frank, I'll not bother you again," Charles said. "You've told me all I need to know."

Charles was certain Dan had received no help from Frank Hampton. Charles was not sure that Dan even knew Frank when they were together in the department. However, at this moment it seemed perfectly clear that this would not have mattered. Trusty old Frank would not have given the younger Dan Carpenter the time of day, let alone help him with the ZB2 specifications.

No, Dan had another source for the specs, he was sure. Beyond that, Charles drew a blank.

Small world, Charles mused. Frank Hampton reporting enquiries to the associate deputy, Andrew Creely. Charles smiled. He could not help wondering how old Andy was doing with *his* dose from Joan Macdonald.

CHAPTER 15

As the date of the Toronto symposium approached, Charles needed a better insight into the latest thinking at the Department of Finance on the R&D support file. It's one thing to know the specific concerns of industry specialists—like the ones from Industry Canada who had bent his ear for nearly an hour. Yet he knew it would be foolish in the extreme to go into a strategic game without a solid appreciation of the broader viewpoint of the department with the heaviest clout in Ottawa.

Charles decided that a conversation with Paul Barton, Director General, Economic Development and Corporate Affairs, was a good investment of his time. He phoned Barton and arranged for a lunch meeting that day. Charles was happy with their agreement to meet at the eastern entrance to L'Esplanade Laurier at noon. It would give him a chance to stretch his legs and to consider, as he strolled, his options regarding Roger Lavigne.

The more Charles thought about it, the less certain he was about what he could do. It was much like the situation he had found himself in when he had wanted to ask Lavigne at lunch whether Dan had ever mentioned working with Portes, and could not come up with a pretext for broaching the subject. How do you ask for details about an event you are not even supposed to know took place? What were his grounds for knowing there was a meeting in Barbados that Dan Carpenter could possibly have attended? And what could his entrée to such a line of questioning be, considering Lavigne had denied Dan's involvement?

The fact Charles was running into a brick wall may have affected his opinion. The view was beginning to form in his mind that Lavigne's statement of denial to Brisson was in reality a side issue, a minor digression of no consequence. Besides, he kept telling himself, he could probably resolve the question, if need be, once he got Dan going on the whole Portes business. Since he planned to do just that in Toronto, and could think of no better alternative, he put the Caper aside once more. He would pay some attention to his job for a change. Rehearsing his agenda for the meeting, Charles hurried to keep his appointment.

Barton's suggestion for lunch surprised Charles. He imagined that a director general in the finance department would come up with one of the old standbys—like Hy's Steak House, as Roger Lavigne had chosen—or Mamma Teresa's, still a hangout for the politicos around the Prime Minister's Office. Barton's actual recommendation came from left field: "Why don't we try the Shawarma Restaurant on the Sparks Street Mall?" Barton suggested. "It's not much to look at, but the Lebanese food is the best in the city."

"Fine with me," Charles replied, noting that he would have a short walk back to his office after lunch.

The two men walked together up O'Connor and along Albert Street. "Ever notice," Barton said as they passed a large government office building, "how pathetic the smokers look these days? Forced out onto the sidewalk, all huddled around the entrances to their buildings."

"Like condemned prisoners shuffling around a jail yard," Charles said.

"Mostly overweight women in baggy shirts hanging out over their slacks, and skinny men in stovepipe jeans and checkered shirts. The support staff of the federal bureaucracy. Wasting half their day away from the job," Barton added with an arrogant sniff.

There, that's more like the stuffed shirt I expected to find in Finance.

After a few blocks, Barton opened the topic of their lunch meeting. He wanted Charles to appreciate the inconvenience of the timing of the Toronto conference from Finance's perspective. Charles, for his part, was quick to assure Barton of his awareness of that issue and stressed that nothing he said at the conference would compromise Finance's position. However, Charles did want to know more about the general approach to tax benefits his department would favour, once the issue was ready for resolution.

As they entered the restaurant, the two officials were deep in conversation. Barton was full of surprises and Charles was pressing him hard for clarification. They searched out a table for two near the window and, choosing without hesitation, continued their exchange, scarcely skipping a beat—except for a momentary lapse on Charles's part. Despite his interest in the argument Barton was laying on him, he could not help noticing the great legs of an attractive brunette seated further up the aisle.

"We don't seem to be on the same wavelength," Barton said, as he dug into his tabbouleh.

"Not really," Charles responded, amused when he considered where his thoughts had been a few seconds earlier.

When the topic of their business conversation was exhausted, Charles turned the conversation to lighter themes: the prospects for the Ottawa Senators hockey team, the sad state of the local newspaper, a touch of speculation on the political future of the Minister of Finance. On these subjects, the two public servants found better grounds for agreement.

As the two officials settled the bill with their waiter, the woman whose legs Charles had recently admired signalled for her cheque. As soon as Haversham and Barton left the restaurant, Lucie Desjardins paid her tab and followed them out the door.

From his vantage point on a mall bench, Rocco Pauli observed the whole scene. It had taken several days for Pauli's contact to check things out. The word had come back that he need not worry about Haversham being tied in with the RCMP or CSIS. What seemed more probable to his cartel contact was that the Canadian authorities were onto Haversham for the same reason that Pauli was on his tail—something to do with the revelation of secrets linked to the drug trade. Even more reason, it was said, to get on with the job and take the son of a bitch out before the police interrogated him.

That broad is sure keeping him on a tight rein, Pauli thought, as he watched Lucie Desjardins pick up Haversham's trail. Making it hard for him to get close to Haversham. Limiting his chances for a clean kill and an unobserved getaway. No choice except to play it cool and await his opportunity. *Watch and wait, that's it.*

From a comfortable distance, Rocco joined the parade. At a leisurely pace, he followed the young agent who, in turn, tailed Charles Haversham up the Sparks Street Mall. It would have seemed a comical sight to the casual observer. Someone ignorant of the deadly seriousness of Rocco's mission.

Chapter 16

1

When Charles's secretary made the travel arrangements, she offered him a choice of hotels approved within the government's travel policy. He preferred the older Plimpton Plaza Hotel, near the corner of Bloor and Avenue Road, close to the University of Toronto conference he would be attending. Although more luxurious hostelries now dotted downtown Toronto, Charles still had a soft spot for the site made famous by many a power breakfast.

"You'll find this is a quiet room," the bellhop said, as he turned on the television set and adjusted the air conditioning. "Your dressing gown and slippers are in the closet, sir. Have a nice stay."

"How late is room service? Charles asked.

"No problem ordering up to two in the morning."

"And what's the hotel's policy on . . . visitors . . . you know, women late at night?"

"I didn't hear that," the young man said with a hint of a leer. "Up to midnight there is no problem. After that, you want to be careful. You should ask her to come down on the elevator from the roof garden bar."

"One good tip deserves another," Charles observed, as he gave the bellhop a generous reward for his service.

"I'm sure you will have a very pleasant stay." Charles noted the smirk again. With a quick pivot, the young man was gone.

Charles placed a call to his secretary. "Hi, Anne," he said, "any news from the home front?"

"Mr. Lavigne called, immediately after you left, but said it could wait until your return. Let me see," she continued, "Mr. Carpenter's secretary also called to verify the starting time of the morning conference sessions."

"That reminds me," Charles said. "Leave my hotel room number with her—it's 721—and ask her to have Dan call me when he reaches the Toronto airport."

"Will do, Mr. Haversham. In fact I'll do that as soon as I'm off the phone."

"Tell her it's imperative that I touch base with him before he reaches the university."

"By the way," Anne said, "you had a call earlier today, and the man wouldn't give me his name. He said that he had the printed materials you requested for distribution at the Toronto conference and could I give him the name of your hotel so he could see they got to you for tomorrow. I told him I didn't know anything about printed materials—I'm sure you would have told me if there were—but he was insistent and, in the end, I told him you were at the Plimpton Plaza. Hope I didn't goof."

"Well, I didn't order anything printed. No bother. Probably somebody wanting to get the jump on letting me know his company's views on subsidies. I imagine he'll show up at my breakfast table tomorrow morning, brief in hand."

2

Charles had expected to end up the day with an agency escort. As he sat at the lobby bar of the Harbour Castle Hotel, waiting for his evening's dinner companion to return, that last resort now looked promisingly distant.

The drinks and appetizers at the reception had been good and the welcoming address by the institute president mercifully short, even entertaining. Better, he had met Debbie Lane, a young woman with whom he had worked as a reporter at the *Toronto Star*. The intervening years, he observed, had rounded the already ample curves of her stunning figure. Time had not diminished the excitement he felt when he was close to her. She also appeared to be much more interested in him than she had ever been when they worked together on the newspaper.

At first, Charles suspected that her warmth—even playful flirtatiousness—owed more to her work as communications director for the Canadian Alliance of Manufacturers, than any real attraction to him as a man. She was, it had to be admitted, attending the conference along with hordes of other "consultants" and lobbyists explicitly to press the case for the industry interests she was representing. He'd seen many times before the insincerity of cocktail party exchanges masked by forced politeness. However, as he had continued to chat with Debbie well away from the swarm of conference delegates hovering around the snacks, Charles became less wary. The thoughts she expressed appeared genuine, her reactions to his comments honest. Charles liked what he saw. Before long he was determined to test how far the chance meeting might lead.

He had begun with an invitation to dinner and had been delighted with Debbie's immediate acceptance. The four-course meal itself had been a smashing success. The hearty Tuscan dishes expertly served at Ristorante Allegro had been delicious. For the main dish he had selected the chicken puttanesca, she the veal ragout with porcini mushrooms and sage. The excellent food was made to seem even better by the house's special young Chianti they had both eagerly consumed.

Their talk at dinner had been warm but essentially nostalgic. It had touched mostly on mutual friends and amusing incidents in the past—reflecting little of their lives in the intervening years. Charles had succeeded once to edge the conversation towards the present, although he had not pursued it, thinking that Debbie preferred to maintain a certain distance. Imagine then his surprise and pleasure at the end of the meal when she had offered to buy him a nightcap at the bar of her hotel.

Charles now watched Ms. Lane walk gracefully into the bar, heads turning as she passed. She had excused herself after finishing her first drink to check her messages at the front desk. Back with the news that no one had called, she was free for the rest of the evening.

"Let's move to a cosy table by the window," Debbie suggested, after she resumed her place on the barstool. "I'd like to get more comfortable, have a quiet conversation."

"I'd like that, too," Charles said, standing close to her side.

"That's sweet," she replied, moved by the warmth shown in his response. "Aren't you hoping this evening will end with more than talk?" she asked, as she reached over to cover his outstretched hand with hers. "Now tell me the truth, Charles," she whispered in his ear. "You must want something more as much as I do?"

Charles did not reply. Instead, he bent down and discretely kissed the nape of her neck.

"I have your answer loud and clear."

"Send our drinks over to that table," he said, pointing the bartender to an empty place in the corner. "We'll have two more Glenfiddichs, no ice, with spring water on the side."

Charles slipped his arm around Debbie's waist and slowly guided her to the table. "And then we'll go up to your room."

3

Charles considered walking back to his hotel. The night was surprisingly mild and he could use some air. However, it was past one and he had to think of the heavy day ahead of him. He hailed a cab and settled in for the short ride.

Debbie had wanted him to stay all night and any other time that would have been his fondest wish. However, as he had explained as tactfully as he could, he needed to be available for Dan Carpenter's phone call from the airport in the morning. He would have to go, although they could be together again that night, Charles had suggested. "Assuming interest on your part," he had added with a sly smile.

Charles did not doubt that his sex partner for the past two hours was as keen as he was on a return match. "Match," Charles now reflected, suggested too much a game. More like a battle, with one side and then the other taking the initiative.

Charles had not anticipated the passion of Debbie's lovemaking. Or his own. Occasionally tender. Often merely efficient. These were his normal experiences with others. However, rough sex—to the point of pain—was new to him. He could get used to it, Charles concluded, as his taxi pulled to the entrance to his hotel.

Charles paid the cabbie and raced through the lobby toward the elevators. He wanted nothing more than to collapse into bed and sleep. In his haste, he completely missed the curvaceous legs on full view from a sofa across the lobby. Lucie Desjardins, who had lost his trail sometime earlier in the evening, had come to Charles's hotel to await his return. An unfortunate lapse in concentration, she would later have to admit, resulting in three hours for which she could not account. For the moment, however, she was determined to look on the bright side: at least she knew where to start shadowing Haversham again in the morning.

4

Although tired, Charles found he could not sleep. His body wanted to accept the role of exhausted sexual athlete; his mind preferred the analyst of human behaviour.

Why was he now uncomfortable—emotionally unsatisfied—as his brain flashed over events of the evening? The searing scratches on Debbie's thighs and breasts, her giving back as good as she got—much rougher stuff than Charles was used to—had thrilled him then. The memory excited him again. Yet in ways that he could not fully explain to the voice arguing in his head, he somehow felt the whole thing had been too easy. Too much of the hunted? Not enough of the hunter? Charles was not sure. Something was missing.

Was it a feeling of guilt, the inner voice asked? Caused by another blatant case of infidelity?

Charles was surer on this one: scruples had nothing to do with it. On this issue, Charles was an amoral pragmatist. Maybe guilt would have come into it years ago—so long ago he could not begin to put a date on it—but not now.

Charles uncovered a parallel between his confusing reaction to his surprise affair with Debbie and the way he had been treating the Barbados Caper. The fact that he thought of Dan's serious trouble as a caper brought home to him the fact that his obsessive concern with what Dan Carpenter had been up to was not driven by any moral judgment on his part. He lacked all motive of retribution or even desire to see restitution. Frankly, even as he learned more of the magnitude of Dan's involvement with the cartel, Charles cared little about legalities or even the propriety of Dan's actions.

Why then was he so deeply committed to his search for truth? Not for truth's sake, Charles now realized, but for the search itself. He was fully absorbed because he had questions for which there were no obvious answers. That the questions kept multiplying only made it more intriguing. Once again, the excitement of the quest, not its conclusion, moved him.

Was this at the root of his reaction to the evening's encounter?

CHAPTER 17

1

Rocco Pauli could have taken a train or a bus to Toronto. A plane was out of the question because of the need to pass through airport security. In any case, he preferred to have his own car available when he was on a contract. It was rigged with a false bottom in the trunk to hide his "tools": knives, a garrotte, a high-powered rifle with scope and silencer, and his favourite—a Colt Python .357 magnum handgun, fitted with a silencer.

Flexibility was his trademark. Born in New York City, Rocco Pauli had become a freelancer with an international clientele. Pauli took pride in his ability to fit the method of assassination to the circumstances. He also liked to work at a deliberate pace, never rushing things. For this reason he had decided to drive to Kingston, stay overnight in a motel, and get out on the road at an early hour. He planned to arrive in Toronto about ten in the morning, after the rush hour and before the midday traffic developed.

Rocco's plan was simple. He would park his car in the basement of a hotel up to two blocks away, then scout out the situation in Haversham's hotel. He could not yet be sure precisely how he would do the job—that would depend on what he found when he established the exact location of Haversham's hotel room and determined how easy it would be to gain entry.

Right now, as he motored well within the speed limit along the 401, he expected he would hit Haversham in his hotel room. The instrument of death would likely be his well-trusted Colt Python.

2

Charles lay on the bed, blankets and pillow piled over his head. He had not heard the alarm clock's gentle ring cycle. The phone finally roused him from a deep sleep. Dan Carpenter was calling from Pearson International.

"Yes, yes, I'm up," Charles growled, rubbing his eyes. "You caught me in the shower, that's all."

"Sorry, but you don't sound wide awake to me. Anyway, you wanted to speak with me before I arrived at the conference. What's up?"

Charles made a huge effort to collect his wits. "I've got a couple of things I need to do first thing this morning away from the conference site," he said, "so the earliest I'd be able to meet up with you would be eleven. I need to bring you up to date on a few things now."

"Shoot."

"It's important you know about a conversation I had with Paul Barton at Finance. It has implications for the general strategy you and I discussed . . . for what we'll say at this conference."

"We were not going to say much of anything, as I recall," Dan said. "And none of it consistent," he added. "I know, too, that Lavigne wants us to do nothing to raise expectations on timing."

"Absolutely right. No change in that. However, Finance is opposed to the tax credit route even for the high-tech industries. You remember we both expected the government would follow the line we favour and try some sort of tax credit approach, while conceding an end to more direct subsidies. Now it appears the line has hardened over at Finance and there's a strong move there to get out of the R&D support business altogether."

"That will fucking never fly," Dan said in his usual understated way.

"I know it won't," Charles replied. "That battle has yet to be fought to the finish. Meanwhile, you and I must say nothing in the next days that will add fuel to the flames."

"Okay. Okay. I understand," Dan said, calming down. "I'll bet Lavigne knew Finance's position all along and said nothing. He wanted to test you. See if you'd check it out for yourself."

"Maybe so. Sure glad I had that lunch with Barton."

"Friggin' ivory tower type!"

Charles changed the subject to the real focus of his day. "We should both show up for the board of director's reception tonight. We can compare notes on who is saying what and spin away to conference participants for an hour or so."

"*No hay problema,*" Dan said.

"What?"

"No problemo, as they say in American movies."

"Good. Then let's sneak off as soon as we can for a bite to eat—just the two of us," Charles suggested.

"Sounds good to me. Shall I try to line up a couple of my exotic playmates, as you like to call them, for later tonight?"

"Ordinarily I'd be keen as hell, but later tonight I have a . . . a commitment I cannot break. By the way, that reminds me," Charles continued, "if you don't have a hotel reservation yet—and it's just like you not to arrange one in advance—you can stay in my hotel room. I won't be needing it tonight, you see."

"You sneaky old bugger. You're getting foxier with every passing year. You can expect to be cross-examined over this at dinner.

"And sure," Dan added, "I'll stay in your hotel room tonight. I'll get a key from you when we meet at the conference."

"Good. See you at the reception, if not before."

CHAPTER 18

1

Charles chose a Greek restaurant on the Danforth for his dinner meeting with Dan. He was sure Dan's love of grilled fish and spit-roasted lamb would overcome any objection he might otherwise have to the restaurant's distance from the conference site.

Charles wanted no interruptions. There was already enough risk that he would not succeed in drawing Dan out on events in Barbados and after. The last thing Charles wanted was to be accosted mid-flight by some association lobbyist or other. Remote enough that even its strong reputation was unlikely to attract other conference participants, the Acropolis Grill was perfect for his purpose. He had merely to await the right moment, and he'd be able to work on Dan without disruption or concern for what might be overheard.

"Let's have a couple of ouzos with our appetizers," Charles suggested, intending to loosen Dan up as soon as possible.

"You go ahead, I'm not fond of ouzo. I think I'll pass for now and have wine with the main dish."

"How 'bout some calamari?"

"Sure."

"And I love taramasalata. It's especially tasty with this fantastic bread. What do you say?"

"Fine," Dan replied, showing no enthusiasm.

"Sure you won't have a beer?" Charles asked, sensing Dan's uncharacteristic restraint.

"Sir, are you trying to get me drunk?"

"My intentions are entirely honourable, worthy gentleman, I simply want you to enjoy this evening and just now you seem . . . well . . . not your usual bouncy self."

"I've had a lot on my mind lately."

"I'm not surprised," Charles said too hastily.

Dan pushed back from the table and stared at Charles. "What the hell do you mean by that?"

"I merely meant that I'm sure it has not been convenient for you to have to break off what you've been doing to help me with this conference."

Dan paused for a minute, weighing his words carefully. "You haven't the faintest idea of what I've been going through. You think it's this fucking silly conference. It doesn't even make my radar screen."

"I know a lot more about what you have been going through than you think."

"Ready to order, gentlemen," the waiter said, as Charles was about to launch into the routine he had been rehearsing in his mind for days.

"Sure," Dan said, grateful to the waiter for the opportunity to collect his thoughts. "Bring me a double gin martini. Then let's go with the appetizers you suggested, Charles. Make that calamari and taramasalata," he said, turning to the waiter. "And I'll have the roast lamb."

Intent on continuing what he had initiated, Charles chose the lamb as well, and—rather than fiddle over the wine menu—ordered a bottle of the house red.

"I know about you and Portes," Charles said, as soon as the waiter left.

"What the hell are you talking about?"

"Look Dan, there's no need to kid me. I know about the deal with the cartel."

Dan's face reddened. He said nothing.

"I found the diskette of your e-mail exchanges with Portes."

"You bastard!"

"It's not something I'm proud of. I got into it when I agreed to look into what they called an inconsistency in your travel expenses for the Auditor General's Office and then one thing led to another. Eventually I established that you were involved with Portes in some way. Then I discovered the Jet Skis, the Spanish CD-ROM and the e-mails between the two of you."

Dan was more upset at the violation of a friendship than the discovery of his transactions with the cartel. "I knew there had to be more behind getting me to this conference than helping you spread bullshit among industry associations. What have they asked you to do? Wear a wire? Commit the ultimate indignity to a friend and trap him into a confession?"

"Believe me, Dan, there is no 'they' at all. I'm not in this for the Privy Council Office, the Auditor General's Office or anybody else. I'm doing this because I want to know everything that happened. I want to understand how a friend like you got involved in this whole affair in the first place."

Dan slumped back in his chair and reached for his martini. He took a deep sip and removed an olive from the glass, twirling it in his fingers before downing it in a single bite. His shoulders sagged. Fatigue covered his whole body like a shroud. Finally he spoke.

"Looking back, I'm not sure why I got involved with Jorge. Who really knows the reasons for one's actions? You appreciate what he is . . . *was* . . . like. A real character. What can I say? I found him exciting—"

"I saw your fascination with him the first time you guys met."

"Jorge was always on the lookout for some type of shady deal, and I found that side of him appealing in a funny sort of way, right from the beginning."

"You kept up a relationship with him?"

"I never saw him again until we both turned up on the task force—I suppose you know all about that, too. However, when we did hook up it was as if we had been lifelong friends. I don't know how to describe it. There was a remarkable meeting of minds. We'd go for drinks together after our meetings and we'd both have a good laugh at the Americans on the committee. We found them so goddamned earnest."

"I know what you mean," Charles said, intent on keeping the story moving forward.

"I remember once telling Jorge that, as a student, I had been totally opposed to the U.S. drug policy of zero tolerance. I simply found it ridiculous, even though I never used hard drugs myself. Jorge said he was of the same opinion. And then we roared with laughter over the irony of the two of us serving on the drug-busting working group."

Dan seemed relieved to be getting his story off his chest for the first time. The stiff martini was beginning to do its work as well.

"A few weeks later," Dan continued, "Jorge e-mailed me to say he had identified an opportunity, as he put it, and wondered if I wanted to pursue it. He said it might fit in with my views on zero tolerance and offer a personal reward as well. I guess you know the rest. Believe it or not, I simply saw it as a bit of a lark at the time."

"A good laugh and some cold cash," Charles prompted. "How much?"

"Enough to cover my debts with some left over," Dan said with a smile.

"Come on, Dan, how much?"

After a long pause, "One mill between us was to be the whole package—that's peanuts for the cartel. But I want you to know that I wasn't in it for the money. Believe me. I was kidding about the debts. I haven't touched a penny yet."

"Mere pocket money, is that what you're saying?"

"Look," Dan said, "I can't speak for Jorge, but for me at least it was something else . . . a risky challenge to get the adrenalin pumping and at the same time give those holier-than-thou Yanks a kick in the ass. I can see now," Dan added after a moment's reflection, "we were not too smart."

"Not very safety conscious, either, judging from what I heard happened to Portes in Miami."

"No. Poor guy!"

"What the hell was he doing in Miami, anyway?" Charles asked. "And why were you supposed to go there to meet him?"

"God damn it, Charles, I can hardly bear thinking about it. That part of my venture with Jorge was classic Murphy's Law at work."

"How so?"

"Jorge had taken an apartment in the Medellin area—the cartel wanted him to be nearby until our transaction was completed. He set up a software program on his computer so we could send digitized information electronically. We had a Spanish soundtrack dubbed onto the CD-ROMs I'd had made for the presentation to the committee, and we were able to get them to our clients immediately and without risk of interception."

"I got that far," Charles said. "Did something go wrong after all?"

"Not with the first stuff I sent, but the cartel asked for more information. I had to go back to the manufacturer for detailed system specifications. It took me a week or so to get this, and—"

"Who helped you get the specs?"

"Nobody," Dan replied without hesitation. "Although the Jet Ski idea was Lavigne's in the first place, by the time I'd finished selling the concept to the task force, I'd made some excellent contacts inside the firm. They were bloody well eating out of my hand when I set up the deal for them. So there was no problem there. Merely a short delay because the chief engineer was on holidays."

"You said Lavigne came up with the Jet Skis?"

"Yes he was keen on including them in the package. The Americans had the original idea about using floatplanes. Cabinet apparently saw an opportunity for Canada to get in there with the orders and instructed us to keep pushing on that front. Then Lavigne called me in one afternoon—I think he'd just come back from some meeting—and suggested I try to get the committee to endorse the notion of adding Jet Skis—Canadian-made, of course—to our shore patrol plan. Suggested, did I say? More like insisted on it."

"Strange kind of issue for Lavigne to get wrapped up in, isn't it? He's usually more concerned with the overall thrust of operations than nitty-gritty details like that."

"That's what I would have said, too, from what I've seen of the man," Dan said. "Not in this case, not at all."

"Who manufactures those Jet Skis anyway?"

"The company is a fairly new kid on the block, Top of the Wave Industries. Apparently, a bunch of guys who used to work for Bombardier broke away a few years ago, got a big load of venture capital from a group of investors, and began to aim at the high end of the Jet Ski business. Very successful. Of course a modest shot in the arm from Industry didn't hurt."

"What did Industry do?"

"You don't remember?" Dan said. "Oh, I guess you were out of our division by then. Andrew Creely's group took a keen interest in the company. They saw all kinds of growth potential and did everything they could to get the Wave—as they liked to call it—

moving forward. Not through direct subsidy. Only a lot of promotional support."

Creely again, Charles thought. Frank Hampton's information made more sense now. Still, it was not evident why Creely, now associate deputy minister, was so paranoid about the ZB2 connection to the department.

"Let's get back to that business with Jorge and his cartel contact," Charles said after another sip of wine. "The cartel wanted you to send more information, and then something went off the tracks. Right?"

Dan nodded agreement.

"What happened?"

"I sent the specs on to Jorge electronically, exactly as I had earlier," Dan said, finishing off his martini.

"Is that where the screw-up came?"

"I don't know technically what happened. I'm no bloody expert when it comes to computers. All I know is that within hours of turning over the information to the cartel, Jorge got a call from his contact. He was furious that the information they received was a garbled mess."

"I'm not sure yet I see exactly how that happened?"

"Who knows?" Dan examined his empty martini glass. "The best we could figure out is that it must have become corrupted in the long-distance data transmission. In his haste to get the information to them, Jorge had not checked the CD, as he did the first time. In any case, the cartel accused him of trying to pull a fast one. Jorge assured them that everything was on the up and up. He couldn't explain it. He promised to set things right as soon as possible."

"I think I see now why you guys planned to meet in Miami," Charles said. "You probably felt you couldn't trust the data lines, so you chose to take the risk of physically handing the information to Portes at a halfway point."

"Jorge wouldn't hear of anything else. He insisted I fly to Miami."

"But you never got there, did you?

"Jorge was scared shitless at this point. He knew his cartel connection was mad as hell. I was doubtful they'd pay us the final installment—and in fact they didn't—but Jorge believed up to the end that we could pull it off. He began to worry, though, that his life might be in danger."

Dan stopped and took a deep breath. "You may not think much of him—or of me for that matter, considering what we've got mixed up in—but I have to tell you, I owe my life to Jorge for keeping me out of Miami when he was worried about his own safety. Within days of his last message, he was dead. The Americans on my working group are almost certain the Medellin cartel got him."

"And what about you? Are you in danger?

"I blow hot and cold on that. Sometimes I'm scared too, and then I calm down and try to get it in perspective. I keep telling myself that, right from the beginning, Jorge was the only liaison. He wanted it that way. He figured he could control the situation better. He also said that if I was to take the risk at this end he'd bear the load at the other. As far as I know, he never told them who his partner was. I am sure he kept it like that to the end. If he did, I'm in the clear. Deep down, I guess I believe nobody in the cartel knows I'm involved."

"And nobody in this country except me," Charles said. "And I assure you, Dan, that's how it's going to remain."

"Thanks," Dan said. He wanted to say more, but a lump in his throat kept him from going on.

The two men ate in virtual silence, exhausted by the tension of their previous exchange. Both paid a lot of attention to their wineglasses. Dan never asked what got the Auditor General's Office onto his case. Or how Charles found the e-mails. Dan was relieved at Charles's assurance that the account of his misadventure would go no further. Otherwise, he felt drained.

The reporter had his story. He had nothing more to ask.

Charles prepared to pay the bill, but Dan would not hear of it. "This one's on me," he said, pushing Charles's credit card back across the table. "I'll pay, you go. I'd like to sit here for a while. By myself."

"Okay. Let's go for breakfast in the main dining room at about 7:30," Charles suggested. "You know, we never did talk tonight about the conference."

Dan rolled his eyes.

"No, I'm not going to get into that now. I can see you're not in the mood. But I still need to know what you've picked up from industry participants today."

"I'll be there for breakfast," Dan said, without enthusiasm. "You're determined to work me up to the last minute of your agreement with Lavigne, aren't you?"

"Damned right, Dan. You may be a touch weird, but you are a great man to have in the trenches. I need your input. See you tomorrow morning."

As Charles rose to leave, he glanced towards the door. Seated at a table near the window was Lester Murray, research director of the institute, who earlier that evening had invited Charles to join him and a few others for dinner. Charles had said then that his migraine was beginning to bother him and he would like to retire to his hotel room. Now he faced the embarrassing prospect of appearing as a liar and—perhaps worse, in these circles—discourteous to his host.

Charles bolted for the washroom before he could be noticed. After a brief stay, he hurried to the kitchen door, shoved a ten-spot in the hand of the first person he met, and slipped through an alley door. Once on the street, he hailed a cab and requested the driver to take him by the fastest route to Debbie Lane's hotel.

Inside, Dan brooded over the evening's surprises. He finished his glass of wine and ordered a Six Star Metaxis. He took stock of his situation.

All the incriminating evidence Charles had discovered was the result of his own foolishness. His perverse addiction to risk-taking had led him to use a computer at work to communicate with Portes and to keep rather than destroy his messages afterwards. A big mistake. No worry. His secret was safe with Charles; he could be trusted to keep his word. And once back in his office tomorrow, he could wipe the entire record, along with all links to Portes's computer.

Dan could not overlook his engagement in a dangerous game of betrayal, with the U.S. government on one side and the Medellin cartel on the other. However, Dan was still confident that the secrecy protocols adopted by the participating countries would protect him. The fact he could count on his superiors in the Privy Council Office to stick to the agreement and continue to deny everything had made him bolder in his venture with Portes.

There was, admittedly, always a chance that the U.S. Drug Enforcement Administration would be alerted to their deal from a source inside the cartel, but, thanks to the warning he had just received, he now had the opportunity to eliminate all concrete evidence that could be used against him. Jorge's death—from Dan's perspective—could also be considered a bonus, removing yet another possible connection that could be traced back to him.

Overall, Dan concluded, the evening was not the complete disaster it had shaped up to be. Although Charles had shaken him to the roots with his unexpected revelation, the situation now seemed under control. He would probably sleep well that night. If so, it would be the first time since he had heard the bad news from Miami.

Dan paid the waiter, left the restaurant and—too tight to get past a breathalyzer test—drove his rented car with extra caution along Bloor Street to the Plimpton Plaza Hotel.

2

"I don't know how it happened," Stan Parker confessed to Lucie Desjardins. "Your man somehow got away without me seeing him. Carpenter has just gone to get his car. We can follow *him*. Slide over and let me drive."

Stan had ordered Lucie to stay in the car. He feared that she had revealed herself to Haversham once too often in the last few days, and the potentially long exposure in the restaurant seemed too risky. Parker, who had gone in alone, had kept his eyes on both men under observation. At least until Charles made his hasty exit though the kitchen.

Parker followed Dan's rented Mazda at a safe distance. When he saw Dan's car enter the hotel parking lot he stopped to let his partner out. "Keep close to Carpenter," Stan said. "I'll park and join you as quick as I can."

Lucie Desjardins entered the hotel a dozen paces behind Dan Carpenter, who went directly to the elevators. She approached the reservation desk, then turned and followed Dan at a safe distance in the same direction. Once the elevator doors shut, she moved closer. She waited until she saw the light stop at the seventh floor.

"He's staying on the same floor as Haversham," Lucie reported to her supervisor as soon as he entered the hotel. "Nothing too surprising in that, is there?" Stan remarked. "And now I know where my man is, I'm out of here. I'm afraid you've no choice but stick around until Haversham gets back. Once you know he's in the hotel, you can pick him up again tomorrow morning."

"You know, life isn't fair," Lucie whined. "You draw Carpenter, the guy the boss is more concerned about. I get the one we're covering only to be on the safe side. What happens? Carpenter turns out to be a pussycat, never gives you any trouble, and what do I get? Somebody who's slippery as an eel. Haversham somehow got away from me last night and now he did it again—to you tonight."

"You've been bitching that there hasn't been enough action for you. Now it looks as if you've got more than you can handle!"

"Maybe we're concentrating on the wrong man," Lucie said.

"That's not for us to decide at this point," Stan said. He was finding the conversation tiresome. It had been a long—and except for the last half hour—boring day. Beneath it all, he was also irritated with himself for letting Haversham out of his sight. Best to leave, he thought, before saying something he would regret. Lucie was a nice girl—an attractive, competent, promising young woman, in fact. Just a bit wet behind the ears. "I'll see you here tomorrow morning," Stan said cheerfully, leaving his junior partner standing alone in the middle of the hotel lobby.

Lucie Desjardins was in something of a quandary. She did not know if Haversham had already returned to his room. Parker had implied that he had not, suggesting that she would have to wait for his return. However, she would feel stupid if he was already upstairs. She could hardly sit for hours waiting for him in the lobby. In fact, she had concluded that—considering her vigil there the previous evening—she would have to find some new approach that night or run the risk of being asked to leave by the hotel detective.

The situation called for initiative, Lucie decided. She could settle the matter with one stroke: call Haversham's room. If he answered, she could hang up with certain knowledge he had returned and then go to her hotel. If he did not answer, she would leave the hotel and continue to observe the entrance from the all night coffee shop across the street. Not bad, she said to herself, hoping against hope that Charles would answer.

"Room 721, for Charles Haversham," Lucie requested from the lobby phone. "Thank you," the receptionist replied, "I'm calling your number now."

The receiver was lifted on the second ring. Lucie was certain she heard a voice, a muffled "Hello." Or was it, "What the hell!" Then a crashing sound as body and telephone hit the floor together. After that, nothing.

Agent Recruit Desjardins was unprepared for this moment, yet she instinctively knew she must act. Her charge was in serious trouble. She had to do something to help, even if explaining her presence would later prove awkward. Without further consideration, she ran to the elevator and took it directly to the seventh floor.

CHAPTER 19

1

Charles opened one eye. For a moment, he had no idea where he was. All he could feel at first was a dead weight pressing down on his chest. His legs felt stiff and sore. His mouth was dry.

Gradually the excesses of the previous evening began to penetrate his memory and he managed a weak smile. He remembered a lot of wine. He also remembered smoking marijuana, something he hadn't done since he had left the *Toronto Star*. Charles felt another positive sign of life returning to the lower part of his half-comatose body as he recalled the deeply satisfying lovemaking that had gone on for what seemed hours.

Debbie, now lying angled across the bed, her head on his chest, had prepared a pleasant surprise for him when he arrived last night. Propped up on huge pillows, cleavage provocatively displayed above the duvet, she had offered an immediate challenge. She had wanted Charles, as she put it with a teasing smile, "to fuck me 'til we're both numb." Struck by the coincidence of this situation and the subject of his serious reflections before he had fallen asleep the previous night, Charles had found the whole thing amusing, but he had overcome his disappointment—again—at not being the initiator.

As he now lay still on the bed, anxious not to awaken his sleeping partner despite the cramp now developing in his left hamstring, Charles came to another realization. Although his wildest sexual fantasies had often run to the rougher kind of sex he had enjoyed the previous night, he now saw that slow and tantalizing lovemaking had brought him far greater satisfaction.

Charles faced a choice. He could try to slip out of the hotel room without waking her, or he could rouse her and say goodbye. Neither option was especially attractive. Leaving without saying anything would appear callous; waking her and then not being able to make love again because of his breakfast meeting with Dan would be frustrating. He preferred to stay the morning. However, the clock was now beginning to press him hard—it was already 6:40—and he was to meet with Dan at the Plimpton for breakfast around 7:30.

Charles chose to leave without further delay. He would shower and change at his hotel. He planned to call Debbie later to explain, confident she would understand.

2

By the time Charles reached his hotel lobby, Stan Parker had been waiting there for half an hour. The agent was as surprised to see Charles enter the hotel as he was not to have already encountered Lucie.

Now Parker was thoroughly upset. Had Haversham left his hotel sometime last night—after he left Lucie in the lobby? Had she tried to follow Haversham and lost him again? If she had lost him, why hadn't she come back to his hotel early in the hope of picking up his trail again in the morning? He needed some answers from Lucie—urgently.

Parker also considered his own situation. Maybe, before he became too carried away with trying to repair Lucie's rapidly deteriorating assignment, he should try to ensure his own case was in good order. There seemed a simple solution to one matter. He picked up a lobby phone and requested the number for Dan Carpenter.

"I'm sorry sir," came the reply, "we've no one registered by that name."

"Try again. That's Dan or possibly Daniel Carpenter."

"I've looked carefully, sir. We have no Carpenter in this hotel. Believe me."

Parker felt cold sweat ooze down the back of his neck as he slowly replaced the handset. His experience had told him there are never easy cases. Some are only less trouble than others. Just as soon as you think you are involved in a cakewalk and let down your guard, something comes along and bites you. Lucie had already been bitten.

His own role in the surveillance was now looking shaky as well. Considering how he had bungled the watch on Haversham last night and failed to verify where Carpenter spent the night, an objective reviewer of his case report might well conclude he was even more culpable than his partner was.

That conclusion was more than enough to galvanize the worried agent into action. He had to cover his butt somehow. He must alert his superiors to the situation and seek their assistance in locating Lucie. Stan pulled out his cell phone and frantically called for help.

3

If he had covered the Toronto crime beat in his days as a newspaper reporter, Charles might have been better prepared when he opened his hotel room door. As it was, he was shocked. Shocked to the point of feeling sick to his stomach.

One body lay on the floor, face down. The other was across the bed, arms dangling, head turned to one side. Charles knew immediately it was Dan, although he had not yet looked at his face. He did not recognize the dead woman.

Charles slumped in the nearest chair, his mind racing. Had the cartel killed Dan as it had done with Portes? If so, how did someone manage to find him in Toronto, considering he had not registered in any hotel? No one—not even Debbie—knew Dan had agreed yesterday morning to stay the night in his room at the Plimpton.

More likely, Charles thought, Dan's death was linked to the woman lying on his bed. She must be a professional Dan had invited back to his room. Did someone who followed her intending to rob them both then kill the two of them? The scenario seemed possible but not probable. Nothing he could imagine made a great deal of sense.

Moving as if in a trance, he reached for the phone beside his bed. He called the front desk and requested the hotel to call the police. "No point in sending a CPR unit," Charles said. "They're both dead." Charles noticed a small hole, ringed with blood, in Dan's back. He also saw the pool of blood that had spread from under Dan's chest. Burying his face in his hands, Charles let the tears flow. He couldn't bear to think of the horrendous damage—what must be a huge wedge blown out of his friend's chest—made by a powerful shell smashing through from the inside.

Charles was still seated on the edge of the bed when the Metro police arrived, two detectives from homicide division and a third man, who did not identify himself.

"Who the hell are you?" the younger detective asked, staring straight at Charles.

"Well, this is really my room, you see," Charles said. "But my friend Dan stayed here last night, instead of me. I came back this morning around seven and found him dead and this woman's body lying exactly as you see her now. I haven't a clue how or why this could've happened."

"And where were you last night?" the older detective said, kneeling now to have a closer look at Dan's wound.

"Do I have to say who I was with?"

"You bloody well better, my friend. He or she may be the only alibi you've got!"

Charles ignored the detective's snide reference to his sexual preferences. He was determined not to be baited into saying anything foolish. He realized he should take his situation seriously. No longer the investigator, Charles was for the time being, at least, their primary suspect in a murder investigation. Deciding to behave accordingly, he offered to tell the police everything he knew.

Of course, Charles reasoned, there was no need to go into the Barbados story or any of the other business with the Auditor General's Office. He explained his work relationship with Dan. He elaborated fully on the reasons for their presence in Toronto and recounted the top line events of their dinner together the previous evening. When he got to Ms. Lane, his information was sparse.

The suspect did not get off that easily. The two detectives were interested in the personal as opposed to professional side of his relationship with Dan. Who were their common friends? Was Dan in the habit of gambling? Did Dan have any enemies (a jealous husband or whatever) who might have wanted to see him dead?

The older detective put the same question to Charles. Beginning with the observation that, were it not for the room switch, Charles might have suffered the same fate as Dan, he asked specifically about Debbie's marital status. The policeman was intent on finding a murder link to motivation along this road. Charles felt he was convincing in closing off that line of enquiry.

The detectives' preoccupation with Dan and himself did not escape notice. There'd been no questioning about the young woman, evidently murdered in his hotel room. The police made no effort to explore her possible relationship with Dan—or with himself for that matter. It was as if they were indifferent to her death—or knew all they needed to know about it from the outset.

Charles found this curious. He was even more puzzled when two ambulance attendants arrived with a gurney and whisked the woman's body from the room without a single word exchanged. There was no coroner's examination. No one bothered to take photographs of the female victim.

Charles saw something else he did not understand. A moment before the paramedics covered the body with a large plastic sheet, the third officer, who had stood silently in the doorway throughout the questioning, moved forward and placed his hand gently on the dead woman's neck. Charles saw him bow his head, then stride out of the room ahead of the stretcher that bore his strangled partner.

CHAPTER 20

1

The rest of the morning was a write-off for Charles. The police finished questioning him shortly after they removed Lucie Desjardin's body from his hotel room. He should stay around, though, for an hour or two for possible follow-up. Meanwhile, they had a number of things to do in his room. The detectives advised him to take advantage of the hotel's offer and move to another floor. There he made a number of phone calls, starting with one to Roger Lavigne.

For a few minutes, the two men shared well-worn sentiments on how deeply Dan would be missed around the office. Then Lavigne switched the subject to the conference. He wanted to know what Charles had learned, who said what to whom, and the extent to which—in his estimation—industry associations' briefs would be able to draw on favourable positions emerging from the proceedings. Charles told Lavigne nothing about his conversation with Dan the night before. Lavigne said he would schedule a meeting between the two of them for early next week.

Charles was quite sure Lavigne would not do it, so he phoned Janet Blair, Dan's secretary, and passed on the sad news to her. Would she spread the word around the office, he asked. Charles wondered if Janet would still be around, if he was able to get back to the office by 5:15 that afternoon. He wanted to return a few of Dan's things to his office, items no longer needed once the conference was over. He did not want them to serve as a constant reminder, he said. She promised to wait.

When he later left his hotel for the university, Charles planned to call Debbie to say goodbye, catch the closing address at the noon luncheon and leave immediately for the airport. He would try his luck on standby and hope to get away from Toronto no later than three.

Charles caught the news on the television in the lounge bar at Pearson International. "Brilliant young Ottawa public servant slain in mysterious hotel killing" was the theme on CTV.

Charles asked the bartender to surf the channels. All the southern Ontario stations were covering the story. Most played up the news that Dan was from the Greater Metro area. A few had somehow already managed to get a picture of Dan at his graduation ceremony. One implied that the handsome bachelor was gay.

No one mentioned the double murder.

Before he boarded the Ottawa flight, Charles made a call to an old colleague in the business section of the *Toronto Star*. The answers to his questions were intriguing enough to cause him to jot down a few notes.

2

Few listeners that day were more captivated by the coverage of the murder in downtown Toronto than Rocco Pauli. Rocco had been working his way back to Montreal through the picturesque side roads of Durham County when he heard the news on his car radio.

Fuck, I only saw him from the back, he thought, but I *know* that was Haversham, not some guy named Daniel Carpenter in the hotel room. What's this crap about Carpenter anyway?

Rocco pressed the "seek" button and caught another station's version of events. Not good news. Rocco tried the radio button again. Even more conclusive detail this time: the victim, they said, was in his early thirties, with blond hair. *The rest of the horseshit doesn't matter. It sure as hell was not Haversham.*

Although Rocco did not know how it could have happened, he now realized—and if he knew, the cartel would know too—he had killed the wrong man. The hit man saw at once he had no choice. He would have to go back and do the job properly.

Chapter 21

1

The traffic on the Airport Parkway was heavier than usual for a Friday afternoon, and nearly everyone had left the eleventh floor by the time Charles got back to the office. Word had spread rapidly among Lavigne's staff that the Old Man had left the office shortly after noon hour. It was remarkable how many found their work schedules permitted an early departure.

True to her word, Janet Blair was waiting for Charles when he arrived at Dan's office. Her mascara still streaked, the frail-looking secretary was having difficulty adjusting to the news of Dan's death. "The second in a month," she whispered as she opened the office door. "First my mother, and now Dan . . . Mr. Carpenter. He was so young." Charles did not intend to be insensitive; he could simply find no reply. "I'd like a few minutes alone in his room, if you don't mind," he said. "I expect you would," Ms. Blair said, full of sympathy. "He often mentioned your name."

Once the door was shut, Charles had no inclination to reminisce. First, he removed the secret cards from Dan's business card box and shoved them deep into his pocket. Then he reached up to the roof of the desk drawer and seized the diskette package. As a final step, he slowly reviewed each drawer—pausing for a wistful smile when he came to the computer games—and then left the desk as he found it, except for the two key pieces of potentially incriminating evidence.

In his office a few minutes later, he wiped the e-mails from the diskette. In the washroom, he flushed the ripped-up cards down the toilet. In no time at all, he was out of the building and on the way home for a much needed drink. It gave Charles a deep sense of satisfaction that he had remained true to his promise to keep everything about Dan's adventure with Portes a secret. Charles was confident his pre-emptive strike would effectively frustrate further investigation.

2

Charles had hoped that he could ease into the story of Dan's death after he had showered and begun to relax with a stiff drink. Diane, who had sent Linda off to a sleepover with a neighbour's child, was ready for him as soon as he opened the front door.

"I heard the news about Dan on the radio," she said. "Terrible isn't it!"

"Incredible!"

"Killed in the Plimpton Plaza Hotel, wasn't he?"

"That's right."

"Isn't that where you usually stay, Charlie?"

"Yes, sometimes," Charles replied, not keen to open up until he knew better where she was headed.

"Where you were staying on *this* visit, right?"

"Yeah."

"Any idea how he was killed?"

"Not really."

Charles moved towards the kitchen. Diane followed closely behind. He poured a couple of generous drinks, adding a small amount of water to both. "Let's sit in the living room," he said, with a weak smile. "Give me a sec for a pee."

Charles could see trouble brewing. Diane was onto something and it likely meant no comfort for him. He desperately wished he knew what details recent news reports had given. Without that information, Charles figured he would simply have to finesse his way through.

Diane was not about to make it easy for him. She hit from an unexpected direction. "Did you talk to Dan before he died?" she asked. "Did he say why he got involved?"

Charles was damned sure he was giving her nothing on this one, especially in view of his efforts that afternoon. He would wipe the trail completely, if he could.

"We spoke, yes, but he denied everything," Charles said, improvising as he went. "I think he must have destroyed his files before he went to Toronto, because he was so bloody defiant. He claimed I couldn't prove anything."

"Did you hit him with the e-mails?"

"Sure I did; he said I had no proof. They were gone, he claimed. Then Dan went on about the lesson he had learned in government was 'deny, deny, deny,' and that though I could say what I wanted or think what I wanted, there was no way he was going to admit to anything."

"Must have rubbed off on you, that line," Diane said, her voice taking on a bitter edge.

"What do you mean?"

"Let me ask you again, Charles. One more time. How was Dan killed?"

"Diane, I don't know."

"Strange isn't it, you don't know, since he was killed in your damn hotel room."

"What gave you that idea?"

"A little birdie told me."

"Come on, Diane, what are you talking about?"

"Come on, Charlie, what are *you* talking about? I've got you dead to rights this time, you bastard. I got a call this afternoon from a guy. Though he wouldn't reveal who he was, he said: 'Ask the old man where Carpenter was killed and watch the bugger squirm. Carpenter died in your husband's room in the Plimpton Plaza last night.'"

"You're kidding!"

"Do I look like I'm kidding? It's true isn't it, Charlie? Isn't it?"

Charles had no response. Not, at least, one that would help much.

"So, if Dan was in your room," Diane continued, her face red with anger, "where the fuck were you? Shacked up with Joan Macdonald, I suppose."

"Oh, for Chrissake, Diane, I haven't got a clue where you are coming from."

"Are you saying Dan wasn't killed in your room?"

"No, I'm not saying that."

"Well, then, were you with that newspaper woman?"

"No. No. A thousand times no. Why in God's name are you bringing up Joan Macdonald? I know her, of course, but I never saw her in Toronto. What makes you think I did?"

"She's worried about you, Charlie Boy. She called here this afternoon. Asked me to have you call her when you got in. The brazen whore!"

"She's only doing her job, Diane. For Chrissake. She's a journalist for the *Vancouver Sun*. She's likely been assigned the Carpenter story. That'd make sense, since she knows the Ottawa scene. I'm sure she just wants to get my version of events."

"Then call her right now, Charlie. Here's the number she left. Talk to her, Charlie. We'll soon see what's what!"

"I'll call her later. I'm going to take a shower first. She'll still have time to file—"

"Phone her *now*, you lying bastard!" Diane made a move from the kitchen. "I'm going to listen in on the extension in the bedroom."

There was no percentage, Charles saw, in procrastinating, although he was not keen to be interviewed at any time by a reporter as sharp as Joan Macdonald. Charles had been lucky enough, so far, to avoid all inquiries from the media. Her story could lead to requests from other reporters and, before long, he would have moved from the shadows to the spotlight—not a particularly happy situation, whatever spin he could try to put on the mysterious circumstances of Dan's death. There was no point, either, in continuing to add fuel to Diane's already raging temper. On the point at issue, he was innocent. So why not call Joan?

Charles dialed the number Diane had given him.

Charles let her phone ring until the voice message came on. "No answer!" he shouted.

"Hold on Charlie Boy. I'm going to try that number myself," Diane yelled, her anger now mixed with frustration.

Charles waited in the kitchen, a fresh drink in hand. He listened for a further eruption. The house was silent.

Minutes later, Diane appeared at the door of the kitchen carrying a small bag. "You're one cool son of a bitch, Charlie. That's all I can say."

He looked at her, puzzled.

"If it wasn't *her* you were with," Diane said, "it was someone *else*. That's pretty damn clear to me." Then she sauntered slowly into the kitchen and took a long sip of Charles's drink, draining the glass.

"I've had it!" Diane shouted. "I want a divorce!"

Now her voice was calm. "I'm taking Linda and going to Mother's for a week. When I get back, I want you out of here. I've finally had enough of your shit."

CHAPTER 22

1

Charles noticed the large black car parked outside his house as soon as he opened the door to leave for work on Monday morning. He didn't expect the driver to be waiting for him.

"Get in and don't ask any questions," a rough voice said, as Charles approached. "I wanna talk."

Charles was surprised, not bewildered. The driver was the officer who left his hotel room with the paramedics.

"Show me some ID before I get in there with you," said a wary Charles. "Show me, or you can take a hike!"

"Don't make me any madder than I am, you son of a bitch," Stan Parker said. "Do as I tell you and get in here now."

Charles did not budge.

"Look," Parker continued in a conciliatory tone, "I promised myself I'd go easy on you. I'm not going to touch you. I only want to tell you something—for your own good."

Now Charles was hooked. He had already figured there was some connection between this guy and the dead girl from the way he had behaved in his hotel room. In fact, by the time Charles had reached the Ottawa airport from Toronto, he had put two and two together and nearly got four. He was certain the dead woman must have been working undercover, likely on something involving Dan's international transactions. That was the only way he could make sense of why the police gave nothing about her to the media. Her affiliation had stumped him, though. Charles had a feeling he was about to find that out, as he opened the passenger door and sat down.

Parker pushed the automatic door locks and turned to face Charles. The CSIS agent's breath smelled of booze. His eyes were black with anger.

"You're a fucking idiot! You couldn't leave well enough alone, could you? You had to mess in where you don't belong. Now look at the result. Your friend Carpenter is dead. I've lost a partner. All because of your interference in something that was none of your concern."

"I have no idea where you're coming from," Charles said, stalling for a chance to think clearly.

"Oh you don't, Mr. Smartass. You don't remember the snoop job the Auditor General's Office gave you?"

"How do you know about that? What business is it of yours?"

Parker's shoulders heaved as the anger and frustration of the last few minutes gave way to a quieter, and more menacing, frame of mind. He looked his captive straight in the eyes. "I know I'm way out of line here," he said, "and this is strictly off the record. But I'm going to tell you something and I'm doing it for one reason and one reason only. I want you to suffer . . . as I have."

"I still don't see what connection—" Charles protested.

"Shut up, you bloody amateur, and listen," Parker snapped as he loosened his firm grip on his prisoner's throat. Charles resigned himself to listening to the speech Parker appeared determined to deliver.

"I work for CSIS," Parker began, "so did Lucie Desjardins, the girl that was killed in your hotel room. More than a month ago, I was told to keep Dan Carpenter under surveillance. I don't need to go into the details of why, let's say that we thought he might have been involved in using information from his government job for personal gain."

Parker did not look like a man who would take well to interruption. Charles bit his tongue. The security agent carried on in one long breath.

"The Auditor General's Office got involved in the act, trying to figure out a mistake in Carpenter's travel expense report. We were interested in any connections Carpenter had with the Caribbean and South America. We found out from the AG's Office that you had been asked to help them out and, when my boss got a report on what you came up with, he didn't like the smell of it and assigned one of our newest recruits to keep an eye on you as well."

"I still don't know why you're so upset with me," Charles said. "What did I do?"

"Damned if I know. Whatever it was, you spooked Carpenter into being real cautious. The guy hardly stirred from his apartment for weeks on end after he went to that Montebello meeting. And you upset somebody enough, with your poking around, that they contracted a hit man to kill you."

"What makes you think someone wanted to kill me?"

"Because Metro Toronto Police arrested the guy last Friday afternoon. Rocco Pauli, a hit man out of Montreal. Caught him hanging around your hotel. He had the same gun on him that killed your friend Carpenter. He refused to answer any questions for a long time. Then when the boys threatened him with first degree murder, he said it was you he was after, not Carpenter."

Parker paused for a moment to let his words sink in. "Of course Carpenter, not you, bit the big one, didn't he? Rocco Pauli must have assumed that Carpenter was you. Not too surprising, eh, considering Carpenter was in your hotel room? And Lucie Desjardins," he added after a pause, "a nice young kid, who somehow became involved, gets killed for her efforts. Sad, very sad."

Charles sat mute as he absorbed the full impact of the message. The disconsolate officer once more filled the void. "To tell you the truth," he said, in a way that showed that all the fight was gone, "what burns my ass is that if we'd had any suspicion that your life was in danger, I would've been handling your surveillance, and Lucie might not have been there at all. If you hadn't given me the slip in the restaurant, none of this might have happened."

More silence. Then Parker said: "And if only I had stayed with Lucie that night, I would have been in charge. I could have handled it, and she wouldn't have been killed."

Charles decided his captor's dramatic turn was now finished. He'd come to deliver his message of pain; it had ended in baring the roots of his own, personal misery.

Charles asked the agent to let him go. Parker said he was free to leave anytime he wanted. However, he had a further measure of discomfort to dispense before he released the car door lock.

"You better watch yourself, Haversham," he warned. "You're not out of the woods yet. Whoever is after you can get another killer to take Pauli's place."

Charles took the full sting of his words and said nothing.

"And, oh yeah," Parker added. "Say hello to the missus for me, will you. I'll bet the two of you had one hell of a fun weekend together, eh?"

Charles got out of the car, adjusted his overcoat and scarf, and continued on his way to the office. Between Stan Parker and Joan Macdonald, Charles had been neatly sandbagged. The outcome, however, was one he was sure he would never have been able to engineer on his own.

2

Trying to dismiss Parker's barb about another hit man, Charles concentrated on the rest of the incident. On reflection, it appeared to have more to do with catharsis for the poor benighted agent, than further investigation of the Carpenter file. Charles had stewed since Friday over the prospect of further questioning about his role in Dan's death. However, the CSIS agent had not actually asked him anything. He had proved to be more in a telling mode. Charles doubted that anybody had a clue how much he had discovered through his probing into Dan's "travel activities."

Charles took this as a good sign. He wondered now how much CSIS had been able to put together on Dan's business with the cartel up to the day he was killed—before Charles returned to Dan's office late Friday afternoon. From the exchange that had just occurred, he assumed not much.

Charles had also been able to dispose on Saturday of his concern over Joan Macdonald's questioning. A phone message left at the number later Friday night had led to a conversation between the two of them early the next day. She obviously knew nothing about the second murder. She never even had the item about Dan dying in what was officially *his* hotel room. Joan wanted human-interest details on Dan's stellar rise in the public service. "A source," she had said, suggested he was a good one to ask. Charles was happy to offer a couple of great quotes.

As he weighed up the balance sheet of positives and negatives— many positives, he now felt—Charles was pleased, too, that he had been able to hold his tongue so effectively in the face of Parker's provocations. All things considered, the restrained approach had worked well to this point. He hoped that his recent run-in was the last he would have with CSIS, and that soon the Barbados Caper would be a distant memory.

There was, however, one piece of unfinished business involving Lavigne. As before, he was not at all sure how to approach it. Lavigne had scheduled a meeting with him for that afternoon and he would find a way—by blunt means or subtle—to get answers to a few questions that continued to obsess him.

By the time Charles reached his office, he had worked himself into an almost euphoric mood. The one dark spot was a nagging image of someone waiting to pounce. Parker's warning stuck in Charles's head as an antidote to his general feeling of satisfaction at how events since Dan's murder had worked out.

He made a pact with his ego to be more careful. Since he couldn't assume CSIS would not continue to watch him, he would avoid situations that might call attention to himself in public. None that involved any kind of risk. He would put Debbie Lane on hold. There would be no more liaisons in Toronto—and certainly not in Ottawa—for a while, at least. Joan Macdonald was now even further off limits.

He would lie low as much as possible. Move out of the Patterson Avenue house into some small and unobtrusive apartment. Life might become boring for a while, but it might in fact make a pleasant change, after the excitement of the past week. Right now, though, he looked forward to his confrontation with Lavigne.

Chapter 23

The meeting set for Monday had been postponed altogether, and the Tuesday rescheduling had been delayed twice by the time Charles entered Lavigne's office late that afternoon. The deputy secretary's absence last Friday afternoon had put his agenda into a chaotic state, and Lavigne was now more irritable than usual. It did not make things better that Charles was trying to brief him on the trade symposium, while his boss seemed more interested in a file he kept picking up and putting down on his desk.

Throughout their unsatisfactory exchange—mostly broken sentences from Charles, grunts and the occasional nod from Lavigne— there was no mention of Dan's death. It is true, Charles thought, that they had talked briefly about the subject last week over the phone. However, it did seem incredible, considering Dan was such a close associate, that his death appeared not to deserve even a passing reference from Lavigne. The papers had said Dan's family had decided on a private ceremony. Charles found the reticence over mentioning this or any related subject unsettling, especially considering the horrible manner and mysterious circumstances of Dan's death. Of course, Charles could have introduced the subject himself, but he wanted to see how the deputy secretary would play the game. It never occurred to him that Lavigne might be doing the same.

Charles continued his account of the Toronto conference. Then, with no buildup, Lavigne leaned towards Charles and said, "CSIS had Dan Carpenter under surveillance."

"Whatever for?"

"I am not sure. I have asked for a report. Received nothing official yet. Two Canadian Security agents tore Carpenter's office apart yesterday."

"Find anything?"

"If they did, they are not saying."

"A CSIS agent came to see me yesterday," Charles said, with no more logical context than Lavigne's earlier one-liner. "He put a number of questions to me about Dan and his responsibilities here,"

Charles added in what was a barefaced lie. "I don't think I was especially helpful."

Although Lavigne did not appear to be listening, that did not deter Charles from pressing on. "The CSIS agent mentioned Barbados several times and wondered if Dan had been sent there as part of his work at PCO. I told him I had no idea, of course. Now I'm curious: why would he keep coming back to that? Was Dan actually ever in Barbados on PCO business?"

Now Charles had Lavigne's full attention. The deputy secretary removed his glasses, fixed Charles with a cool stare, and picked up the phone. "Have Fred Harris come into my office immediately." He looked back at Charles, drumming the desk with his fingers. "Interesting coincidence," Lavigne said, his tone now sarcastic. "André Brisson, from the AG's office, called me one day and asked me the exact same question."

"What did you tell him?" Charles asked.

"I told him Carpenter never attended any meeting in Barbados."

"And was that the truth?"

"Damned impertinent of you to ask, don't you think, Haversham?"

"Well, I have reason to believe—"

The door to Lavigne's office swung open to reveal an ashen-faced Harris, eyes darting back and forth between Charles and the boss, uncertain as to whether he was on the right page—or even in the right act.

"You were right, Fred," Lavigne said. "It looks as if Haversham here is our leaker. Good work. He has some explaining to do to us now."

Harris, more comfortable now, sat upright in a chair to the left of Lavigne's mahogany desk and watched intently for Charles's reaction to the challenge.

"I don't know what you are talking about. Leaker?" Charles said, figuring that defence was the more appropriate strategy at this point.

"Do you deny that you received a special delivery package from the Auditor General's Office?" Harris demanded, enjoying the moment of authority. Charles searched for a reply, but Harris went on. "I suppose you also deny that you found an excuse not to meet with the rest of us at Montebello? And that you visited the office that weekend to snoop on Dan Carpenter?"

"I did go to the office on the Saturday, that's true. I went to get some work to take home. I expected I might be away from the office on the Monday—because of my daughter—and I had something important I was working on."

"Then what were you doing in Dan Carpenter's office?" Harris asked.

"What the hell do you mean?"

"We've got you on videotape, old boy. The video never lies!"

"This place has a video surveillance system, too?" Charles asked, beginning to sound desperate.

"I had it installed for the weekends," Harris said proudly. "You're not the first in the office to forget where their loyalties lie."

"Loyalty is extremely important to me," Lavigne said. "It is the cornerstone of the Privy Council Office."

"Does that include hiding the truth from an auditor general?" Charles demanded, risking going on offence. Defence had not served him well thus far.

"If you are talking about that Barbados business, I say absolutely," Lavigne responded. "You don't think for one moment I was going to give another club to the Auditor General to beat the government with?"

"I don't follow you," Charles said.

"I suppose there's no harm now in explaining," Lavigne said, looking at Fred Harris in a way that suggested they were working to a script.

"If you had been in the office at the time," Harris said, "you would have known we had only recently put the travel expense brouhaha out of the way before the Office of the Auditor General contacted you."

"It was risky enough that we had to misrepresent Carpenter's travel expenses to the committee meeting in Barbados," Lavigne said. "I was in no mood to open the door to any more probing."

"I don't understand what was so special about the Barbados meeting," Charles said.

Again, the two men exchanged glances. Harris was the one to speak: "That particular meeting was a full session of the task force. The industry minister wanted to lend support to Carpenter's presentation. So, he attended along with the assistant deputy minister of the department. A couple of the minister's staff went, too—mainly for the golf, as I recall."

"I had no desire to see the top level of Industry Canada caught in a new, and even more sensational, expenses scandal," Lavigne added.

"I can't believe that all your secrecy and deception was simply to cover up for a couple of ministerial staff," Charles said. "Surely, the minister's presence and even the ADM's was legitimate government business. As was Dan's. What was the worry?"

Lavigne looked at Harris, who was now staring at the floor. Charles opted to press further.

"Might your intention to mislead also have had something to do with your personal interest in the equipment Canada was trying to sell to the task force at that meeting?"

This time there was no eye contact between Lavigne and Harris. The deputy secretary grew red in the face. Eyes blazing with anger, he turned to Fred Harris: "Leave us alone, I'll call you if I need you."

Harris slunk from the room.

"You're a nasty a piece of work, Haversham," Lavigne sneered, as soon as Harris was gone. "What can one expect anyway from a man whose entry into the federal public service took place in such an unfortunate—not to say, sleazy—manner?"

It was Charles's turn to show surprise and anger. "So it is true," he said, the final bit of circumstantial evidence he needed slipping into place. "You do know Seymour Bart!"

Lavigne's eyes narrowed to slits. He remained silent.

"Only one person," Charles continued, "knows the story of how I got into the civil service. Seymour Bart. It's his consortium that holds a controlling interest in Top of the Wave Industries, isn't it? The firm whose product you insisted Dan peddle to the task force."

"I had absolutely no personal interest in the sale of any of those Jet Skis."

"No personal interest maybe," Charles said, his voice rising. "But more than a little concern for the success of the venture, isn't that so? For the sake of your standing in 'The Group'? Repayment of a favour to the persuasive Professor Bart? A guarantee of extra security in your retirement years? Which was it?"

No response.

Charles pushed again. "It was, in fact, your personal involvement in the Jet Ski business you meant to cover up by pretending that the Barbados meeting never existed, whatever poor Harris may think is the pretext."

"I don't have to defend myself against a man like you," Lavigne said. "A man so bereft of character that he was willing to betray a friend by snooping on him."

"You are hardly the one to lecture me about principled behaviour," Charles said.

"Perhaps not," Lavigne said. "However, I am the one in authority and you are not. It will be my judgment that prevails, Haversham. And don't you forget it."

"So, there will be no move to the Langevin Block for me, I take it."

"Not in my lifetime."

The deputy secretary picked up the red file from his desk and glanced at the first page. He cleared his throat. "In fact, your services are no longer useful to this office," he said. "We consider you too great a security risk."

"Security risk! You're going to dump me?"

Lavigne handed Charles a sheet of paper from the file. The typewritten report of the Metropolitan Toronto Homicide Division, directed to the Deputy Secretary (Operations), Privy Council Office, filled a page.

> Charles Haversham, a resident of Ottawa, was interrogated by Detectives Browning and Norris on suspicion of being an **accessory before the fact** in the MURDER of Daniel Edgar Carpenter, also of Ottawa, and Lucie Anne Desjardins, of no fixed

address. Based on the testimony of the suspect and the perpetrator, Rocco Pauli, also of no fixed address, NO CHARGES WILL BE LAID against Haversham.

Pauli claims that Carpenter's death was unintentional; that he planned only to rough up Haversham; and that he choked Desjardins when she surprised him in the hallway. The arrested man denies premeditation.

Our investigations provide no direct evidence on Pauli's motive. Apart from some references to being under orders, he has refused to explain his presence in Toronto or his actions. Interviews with hotel staff indicate that Haversham was planning to engage the services of prostitutes during his visit. We have not ruled out the possibility that the threat to Haversham's safety was sex-related. The suspicion remains that Pauli's assignment to hurt (or kill) Haversham may be explained by the latter's irregular record in matters of this kind.

Finally, we wish to report that it is the opinion of CSIS Agent S. Parker, who has assisted us with our work, that Charles Haversham's lifestyle makes him a target for blackmail. He therefore represents a POTENTIAL SECURITY RISK.

"You don't believe that police college nonsense, do you?" Charles said, searching his mind for an angle to counter the damaging report.

"It hardly matters, does it?" the deputy secretary replied. "I have their report and it will serve our purposes nicely. Better, I am sure, than the grounds for dismissal we had already prepared before receiving it. On your way out, see Harris. He's prepared your letter of resignation. Fill in the date and sign it."

"By God, you play hardball," Charles said, as he moved toward the door.

"I'm simply doing what I have to do," Lavigne said.

"Merely another case of 'needs must,' I suppose," Charles said.

"Quite so," Lavigne replied. "Plenty of those situations these days."

CHAPTER 24

As far as the neighbours were concerned, Charles Haversham was at home because the office had granted him leave of absence to recover from the shock of a colleague's death. Charles meant to enjoy the break, rather than torment himself over the actual cause of his forced retirement; it was not in his nature. A feeling of guilt over causing Dan and another's death now joined fear for his own life.

It was bad enough to face a possible threat; to have no explanation for it made the sensation all the more eerie. Charles was grateful he could remain indoors. He often caught himself looking out the window to survey the street.

In the first days after Dan's murder, relief at his own survival—then Diane's dramatic blowup—had obscured the reality that, through misadventure certainly but by his own actions nonetheless, his friend had been killed.

Though consoled by his destruction of the evidence—a move he could now rationalize as an extension of his promise to Dan to keep his secret safe—Charles was now preoccupied with a feeling that this virtuous action after death failed to compensate for the disloyalty he had shown while Dan was alive. No degree of intellectualizing would soothe Charles's regret that his ill-judged acceptance of Brisson's request for assistance—and, of course, his own headlong drive to satisfy curiosity over Dan's Barbados Caper—were contributing factors to the tragic events in the hotel. Were it not for wanting a session alone on the Jet Ski business, Dan would not have been in Toronto at the time. The contemplation of these facts made Charles miserable.

When he came to Lavigne's actions, Charles was remarkably dispassionate. In the first hours after the encounter, he had been livid, taking his anger out in the first bout of heavy drinking in over a month. However, in a period of sober reflection afforded by his comforting den, Charles later accepted that the outcome was about as good as he could expect.

Lavigne and Harris had caught him flat-footed on the disloyalty issue. (Charles did not ignore the larger disloyalty issue altogether—Lavigne's own culpability in a breach of public trust. However, once again, his reaction was more surprise than critical judgment.) Charles accepted that, once the deputy secretary's antennae were activated, it was merely a matter of time. That bastard Harris, after reviewing videotapes, had obviously called for the standard office logs on incoming and outgoing mail and had spotted the suspicious origin and timing of the hand-delivered package from the Auditor General's Office.

Lavigne, for his part, had done his best to keep Dan away from the office to minimize the risk that someone might try to draw out information from Carpenter that they could link to the Barbados meeting. Once the "leaker investigation" (Lavigne's idiosyncratic usage that Harris no doubt felt obliged to adopt, too) targeted him, Lavigne had only to wait for confirmation from the lips of their prime suspect. Charles noted with chagrin that he'd sealed his own fate with a ruse that had backfired, one he'd devised to draw Lavigne out on his lie to Brisson.

"Confidence in one's subordinates is the necessary if not sufficient condition for good administration," Lavigne liked to say. It was a rule Charles understood Lavigne would live by, without exception. When he fell short of the standard, they axed him.

Charles appreciated that, in the end, he had been chopped, not executed. Although the convenient report of the Metro Police may have strengthened Lavigne's determination to fire him, the skillful commander recognized the double-edged sword he was wielding. In a battle over wrongful dismissal, neither side would relish providing the evidence that would inevitably be required to make the case— in either direction. A standoff, a face-saving exercise for both sides, seemed the most appropriate solution. This the two parties agreed to in Charles's letter of resignation.

Terms were set under which Charles could be transferred, if he so wished, to the staff of the Institute for the Study of International Trade and Investment, a small Ottawa think tank funded mainly by Foreign Affairs and International Trade and Industry Canada. Although the deal gave Charles a job he could go to each day, he knew he was at the end of the road in his climb to the top of the Ottawa mandarinate. At least as long as Lavigne was around to thwart him.

Charles felt he would soon not regret losing the position he had held for such a short time in the Privy Council Office. He could predict with assurance, however, that the blow to his ambition to succeed in Ottawa would fester inside him forever.

Charles had slept heavily the first night after his dismissal, aided by nearly a full bottle of Scotch. The next two nights proved more fretful, his sleep interrupted by recurring nightmares, in each version of which the motif of Charles desperately trying to crawl his way up a long, mud-soaked embankment reappeared. Sometimes he was trying unsuccessfully to drag along a person he had rescued from a river; in other cases, he was just trying to save himself.

This night Charles would avoid nightmares by the simple expedient of not attempting to sleep. Instead of tossing for hours only to awake in panic when he did fall asleep, he planned to read, watch a late movie on television, play a video if necessary— anything to distract him from the conflicting feelings that worked away inside him.

He picked up the *Ottawa Citizen*, unread from the morning, and aimlessly turned the pages of the want ads. He glanced at a few entries under professional vacancies and went on to the travel section. The theme of the issue was "Fun in the Sun." "Spend Christmas in the Islands," the travel editor urged. "Relive Summer in Tobago," another breathless bit of prose insisted. Charles stayed with the topic, enticed by the photos of gorgeous island girls in scanty bikinis.

He was surprised at the price of some of the holiday packages. You could get to Miami, he noted, for next to nothing. But Caracas or Buenos Aires cost a fortune. How much would a regular flight cost? Worse, what would one have to pay for business class? What, for example, was the travel bill for Dan's party of five for a premium flight to Barbados?

Charles closed his eyes and reflected on the fact that this was the first time in at least three full days that Dan's part in the Barbados Caper had even crossed his mind. What had until recently been his almost total obsession had been pushed from the scene by his own crisis. Now that he had worked through his reactions to Lavigne's decision, he felt more inclined to return for a moment or two—in his mind at least—to his old agenda.

Charles lay back on the couch, his head heavy with fatigue, and let his recollections rewind to the night he had worked out his "who, what, where, when and why" assessment of Dan's mysterious actions. Charles felt a small tingle. He was moving outside himself, regaining a concern for a question larger than his personal predicament. He was curious now about how accurate he had been at an early stage in his "investigation," considering what he learned since that time. Charles thought it might be fun to check.

He moved to the den and opened his left hand desk drawer that held his Caper file. The notes he had hidden there appeared even less substantial than he remembered. He kicked himself for not writing more legibly. More detail would also have been useful. Still, he could make out the main points of his "to do" list and, after a quick read, was satisfied he had followed through on everything of importance recorded then. He paused to give himself and Mark Gilmore a congratulatory pat on the back for guessing that the unidentified computer access number was in fact not to Dan's office computer. That, he recalled, had turned out to be the critical link to Portes's computer in Colombia.

What an ass! He had been so pleased with his success in establishing a phone link to Portes's computer that he had completely forgotten about the other Medellin area phone number he had rung. Although he wasn't sure how it had happened, once again Charles saw he might have been his own worst enemy. One of the unanswered phone calls he had placed from the phone in his den must have put the cartel on to him rather than Dan. Of course. Dan had told him that Jorge handled everything, kept the cartel in the dark about Dan's identity. Charles now thought of Stan Parker's remark about a second hit man in a new light. *Oh my God, the cartel must still think I'm Jorge's partner.*

More than a tingle this time. His heart now pounded with fear.

After a few deep breaths, Charles slowly regained his composure. A slight tremble still evident in his fingers, he strained to put some order to his notes.

Charles was especially interested, in retrospect, in the evidence he had collected for thinking Carpenter and Portes were involved together. If the Medellin cartel did not know it, how exactly had he made the link? He paid closer attention to establishing the chronological order of the sheets of paper spread out on his desk.

Much of the basis for his early opinion, he now saw, was circumstantial and incomplete. Charles did pick up one thing, however, that—although considered significant at the time—had been forgotten in the interim. It was enough to fire another shot of adrenalin through his body.

What had given him his first strong indication that Dan and Jorge were involved in a venture involving personal gain? Charles reconstructed an answer from his jottings: password created from their initials, numbers linked to an account. Mark had said they could be for a credit card. However, that was before Charles found the e-mails and confirmed the payoff from the cartel. No, those numbers belonged to a bank account. Without question.

How could I have so easily ignored this important fact? Now, where in hell are the access codes?

The numbers and letters, Charles remembered, were on separate cards, as he had seen them for the first time in Dan's office. He had used the two phone numbers since then—*damned right he had*. Where were the others? Had he kept copies of all the cards?

Nothing visible in the file.

Charles ripped through the drawer where he had stored his notes. All he accomplished was to turn everything topsy-turvy. He needed a better approach. Calming himself, he dumped the contents of the desk drawer on the floor. The cards, which had slipped out of the file folder onto the bottom of the drawer, now rested on top of a pile of clippings, notes and assorted papers.

Laying the cards out on his desk, Charles looked at each in turn, and then set three aside. With elaborate ceremony, he placed two cards face up in front of him and sat back to admire:

JRPDEC2

7890 9811 0022 4598

A silly grin spreading over his face, he switched the cards and enjoyed the new result all over again:

7890 9811 0022 4598

JRPDEC2

The simple pattern—formed by the bank card number and what he was convinced was the password—was quite beautiful. As he frantically shuffled the two cards around, back and forth, he suddenly felt giddy—even intoxicated. He could feel the pain of the past days easing from his body. An old sense of excitement gripped him.

Charles felt like smiling. So he smiled. Then he laughed. Not a tiny snicker of a laugh, but a full, deep belly laugh that nearly brought tears to his eyes. He saw relief for his present predicament around the corner.

He could not stop smiling.

What a lovely gift! What a bloody lovely gift! Thanks, Dan and Jorge. Thank you both for your generous contribution to the Save Charles Haversham's Bacon Fund.

He would start immediately to experiment with different online banking sites until he hit one that Dan's codes could access. He wouldn't be able to transfer Dan's funds to his own account—not without more security information than he had now—but he was certain he could use the online account to pay some hefty bills. Wasn't that well timed?

For the moment, Charles favoured the notion that a single ticket for a round-the-world-trip was a good place to start.

ABOUT THE AUTHOR

An Enemy in View is the first novel from an author who has been doing other types of writing for the better part of his life. A former professor of political science, federal public servant, and, for nearly two decades, partner in the Ottawa office of one of Canada's leading social research firms, David Hoffman turned to novel writing in his semi-retirement.

Born in St. Catharines, Ontario, he grew up in Hamilton and, since then, has lived in Toronto, London (England), Glasgow, Montreal, and Ottawa. Readers will find in this suspenseful story evidence of his acquaintance with the Ottawa bureaucracy, his geographic mobility, and his love of fine food. Married with five grown children and step-children, he lives in Ottawa's downtown, within an easy walk of the locations that play so prominent a part in his book.